The

# Claude Glass

**Claude glass**, *n. phr.*: a small convex mirror of blackened glass. Used widely by tourists and artists of the late 18th and early 19th centuries, its miniature, muted reflection would render a view 'picturesque' – that is, like a picture, and particularly like the idealised landscapes of Claude Lorrain (1600–1682).

*For C*

*O blesséd vision! happy child!*
*Thou art so exquisitely wild*

William Wordsworth,
To H.C., Six years old.

# CHAPTER ONE

# A WORLD OF LINES
# AND CIRCLES

The rain fell endlessly in Radnorshire. It came in lines across the hills – blown against the walls of the barns at Werndunvan, oozing through the weatherboards and pouring through the holes in the roof. Across the farm, every sheep path, every ditch and furrow, became a stream, until the hillside was a web of water and thick brown arms reached from the edge of the bottom field into the pond on the edge of the forestry beyond.

Sitting between the big, open doors of the barn, Andrew would look out at the lines and the circles in the puddles. Pressed around him, the dogs nipped him and nuzzled him to play – warm, damp and sharp-smelling – but Andrew stroked them almost without noticing, staring across the yard where the circles shimmered

1

between the house and himself, between the footprints of the cattle and the ugly brown ruts of the tractor. They were so beautiful that a dizzy feeling rose up in him, like he felt when he was going to sleep, and it was as if there were nothing but these lines and circles, spreading away from him as far as he could see.

That December, the cold weather came early, freezing the damp ground and leaving its teeth along the guttering. The mud was hard in the yard when Andrew's father, Philip, collected him from the barn and the two of them rode on the red Massey Ferguson, down the hill, past the pond, and right into the heart of the forestry plantation. To the north, to the south and west, lines of pines surrounded the farm, and as Andrew watched from the box on the back of the tractor, curled among the dogs, tunnels would open between them and close again just as rapidly – each one shrinking away towards the bottom of the world. He watched them, fascinated, mumbling as Meg licked his face, his head held back against the side, away from the sleet that melted on his cheeks and spilt around the cab of the tractor.

Across the ice-fringed puddles, Philip took the ladder and leant it against one tree after another. He took his muttering chainsaw and climbed to the highest rung, slicing off the top few feet, which fell to the ground as a Christmas tree. Right across the plantation, Andrew could see where his father had performed the same operation in previous years, where clusters of pines were either brown or skeletal, where moss was crawling upwards from the ground to coat their few remaining branches.

It had always amazed Andrew that you could get a small tree, simply by cutting off the top of a big one.

\* \* \*

A few days later, Philip called Andrew again from the barn, but this time, instead of riding on the tractor, they drove down the track on the springy brown seats of the car. They passed among the frost-coloured fields, through gates and over cattle grids that purred beneath the wheels, until, to Andrew's amazement, they came to the lane that flowed down the valley and all the way into the village. Climbing onto his knees to peer outside, for the first time in his life Andrew saw taut new fences, a line of houses with splashes of light and colour in the windows, a field full of stones and, beside it, a building so tall that it came to a point among the dark, snow-heavy clouds. Andrew pressed his face to a space in the icy glass, watching the giant building for as long as he could, but his father turned off the road onto a small slope between two pools of grass. He came to a halt outside a square red house and, without a word, climbed out of the car and vanished away around a corner.

Left on his own, Andrew began to feel scared. He sniffed at the smells of the dogs on the hair-scattered seats and he stared at the place where his father had vanished, longing for him to reappear. But then he heard a noise from behind him – a chorus of voices, like ewes pressing through a gate – and, keeping his head as low as possible, he peeped over the seat-back to see what on earth it could be.

Just beyond the turning, there was a red and grey building in a big black yard surrounded by a jagged stone wall. And out of the building's front door were streaming, not sheep, but other children like him. They were pawing and pushing, dancing and jumping, breaking into groups and chasing each other across the yard, and together they were making such a racket that Andrew couldn't make out a single individual voice. So intently was he listening to them that he didn't even hear his father until he pulled the door open and climbed heavily back into his seat, tossing a bagful of small brown bottles onto the floor. They were the type that his mother kept on top of the television. She would open them often, tipping white dots onto her palm and staring at them blankly.

"Fucking doctors!" Philip growled. He started the engine, and pebbles went flying up behind them. "Think they know fucking everything!"

They had scarcely turned the next corner before they stopped again, this time next to a white-walled house whose door was framed by blinking, colourful lights. Snow was floating through the cold air, settling like dust on the potholed ground as Andrew followed his father into a hot, dark room full of smoke and the sickly smell of beer, where men in overalls glanced at them in a way that made Andrew want to run back outside. Here, Philip continued to look angry – his forehead ploughed and pressed together – and, clambering up beside him on a stool as tall as himself, Andrew tried to look just the same, pulling his brows together and hunching his shoulders. In front of them there was a wall of shiny wood that he could just see over and, behind it, a woman with black hair and bright red lips was smiling at him as she pulled on a long white handle. She handed two fat glasses of cider to Philip, one of which he pushed towards Andrew, who soon started to play with it, dipping an old pipe that his father had given him into the foaming brown liquid and spilling it onto the wood, watching as the droplets shrank and twisted into tadpoles, dogs and dragonflies.

"Honestly, Philip. You are an old miser!" the woman laughed, her voice shrill and uncomfortable. "Can't you at least buy this boy some decent clothes?"

"That's enough, Branwen!" barked an old man, who was sitting near the fire. "You keep your bloody nose out of it!"

For a moment, Andrew looked at the two of them, sucking on his empty pipe, wondering why they sounded upset, but then he realised that they were talking about him and he hid himself beneath his father's old cap and buried his arms inside his jacket. Beside him, he heard Philip gulp down his cider, slam down the glass and reach for the other. Around him, the room was so quiet now that he could hear the whispering of the fire, the rumble of a tractor outside on the lane, and he understood that it was his fault that they were all so angry. He sat on the stool in his dog-shredded jumper, the sleeves spilling down over his hands, in the cut-down, filth-smeared trousers that, like most of his clothes, had once belonged to his father, and all that he wanted was to be back in the barn, to be curled up with the sheepdogs, among the bales and the sweet, sharp smells.

\* \* \*

Across the hill at Penllan, the snow drifted over hedges, changed the shape of the valley, added contours and covered streams where shining contortions of ice had hung between the banks for weeks already. The ponds froze until you could walk right up to the water-hole where the ducks kept plugging around in circles, and would burst into the air if you came too close – flying in their tight formation, landing again cautiously so as not to scoot across the ice on their bottoms and crash into the opposite bank.

The blizzard continued for three days and nights, bursting the pipes in the walls of the bathroom so that water poured through the floor into the kitchen, which duly flooded and turned into an ice-rink in the boot-passage. The thin black branches of the trees vanished into the all-eating whiteness. The sheep abandoned their feeders for the shelter of the hedgerows or the old quarries up on Cold Winter, huddling together in precisely those places that were most likely to be enveloped by a snowdrift. So Adam and Tara locked the sheepdogs in the house and crawled with torches out across the snow, feeling with their hands for the half-frozen animals and driving them tottering into the relative warmth of the big shed.

In the pool of heat in front of the woodburner, Robin and Martin were playing with a multicoloured castle. They had a blue and white police car that Robin, the older boy, was driving round the hearth rug, out across the floorboards where cold air rose in plumes from the cracks, and they had an evil army of tractors and soldiers that was waiting for the order to attack.

"Robin!" said Martin. His lower lip was beginning to jut forwards. "Robin, I want to play with the police car now! I want to fight the Sheenah army, too!"

In the shadows of the drawing-room, the two boys might have been different-sized versions of one another. Robin was taller, paler and skinnier, but both had blond fringes that stopped neatly at their eyebrows, and both wore the red and green dressing-gowns that their mother had made for them, tassels swinging from the hoods. At a glance, you might have missed the green intensity of Robin's eyes, or the stubborn specks of colour that were growing on Martin's plump cheeks.

The drawing-room was the province of the grown-ups, a place of shadows and mystery, and it was an honour to be allowed in here at the best of times – let alone to be left with the toy box, a cup of hot milk and a flapjack for each of them. It was the room of locked drawers and cupboards full of photographs, the television, banks of dusty records and other such fascinating things. Across one wall, there was an enormous bookcase that had been built by their father, while other walls were covered in pictures of dancing skeletons, fire-covered monsters and – Robin's favourite – a lady with an extra eye in the middle of her forehead, floating above a range of snow-topped mountains.

"Robin!" Martin repeated, his lip trembling. "Robin, it's my turn now!"

Once his brother had started crying, Robin pushed the police car away across the carpet and jumped up onto an armchair, leaning against the back and staring at the floating lady. The lady had very white skin, with flowers in her hair and a pleasant smile, and she had a comforting quality about her that reminded him vaguely of their mother. The world where she lived was a world full of wonders – people with numerous arms and dragons with the faces of tigers – and Robin smiled back at her as his thoughts wandered off among the mountains and the spiralling clouds.

Beyond the thick stone walls, the wind drove against the open hillside, sucking and gasping in the chimney and rattling the windows in their sockets. It stirred the hems of the heavy green curtains and excited the firelight, but Robin paid it no more attention than he did Martin, driving the police car across the carpet with waning enthusiasm, or the sheepdogs, who had never even been inside the house before, pressing their noses to the crack beneath the door to the boot-passage, whimpering to be allowed back outside.

\* \* \*

Adam worked every day of the year except Christmas. Every morning, long before Robin had even woken up, he was away in some distant part of their eighty-seven acres, his flat cap pulled down over his sandy hair and his weather-lined forehead, his wide shoulders hunched into a fake Barbour jacket and his pockets full of straw, fencing staples, baler twine and holes. When Adam walked, he strode, the dogs trotting dutifully behind him. When he knocked in a nail, he used a couple of giant blows, and he could pick up a bale with one hand and toss it onto his back as if it were hardly there at all.

Robin could remember only one occasion when Adam had left the farm for more than the few hours that it took him to go to the markets in Abberton or Hereford. Early in October – not long after Robin's seventh birthday – a man called Owl had materialised in a pale blue van with a back like a half-timbered house. He had stayed with them for a whole month. Owl was huge, with an enormous golden beard and hair in a ponytail that came halfway down his back. He was one of those grown-ups who always seemed happy to come outside and build roads up mountains in the sandpit or to sail paper boats on the puddles. The problem was, you could rarely find him awake – he was often in bed until it was almost dark – and sometimes Robin would hear him early in the morning, sitting on the lawn, playing his guitar, smoking and watching the sunrise over the sinuous back of Offa's Bank.

One day, Owl was in the yard when Robin was going to school, his head beneath the bonnet of the van while Martin stood beside him, holding the oilcan and asking to be lifted up so that he could see what was going on.

"I'm just fixing up this old banger," Owl told Robin, tapping his cigarette onto his jeans and rubbing in the ash with his fingers. "The blasted carburettor's on the blink, and me and your dad are supposed to be going to this car auction off near Gloucester."

He sat down in the driver's seat and turned the key several times, but nothing much happened, except for a few pops and bangs from the exhaust pipe, so the three of them went down to the ruts at the bottom of the yard and built a mud city, complete with stick bridges, waiting for Adam to come along with his toolbox and get the van sputtering into life.

That evening – when Robin and Martin were sitting at the kitchen table, drawing pictures of men in peaked hats shooting one another – there was a bellowing noise on the track and the house seemed to start shaking, light blazing through the curtains in the living-room. The two boys ran around the path by the back door, squeezing between the bars of the gate, and they arrived in the yard to find an enormous blue truck rumbling to itself in front of the barns – its bonnet bulging and its headlights lighting up everything from the muddy puddles to the alarmed-looking bantams on the beams in the hayloft.

"Boys!" called Adam from the window, and the truck made a noise like thunder. "What do you think of that, eh? Get your mother down to have a look!"

The two of them remained where they were, gawping, unable to move in any direction until Tara arrived and led the way past Owl, whose feet were on the dashboard, through the glare of the headlights, the oily reek of the engine, to the door, where Adam was just jumping down to the ground.

"Adam?" asked Tara quietly. "How on earth are we supposed to afford this thing?"

"It's okay," he smiled a little sheepishly. "Honestly, love. The auction was great! They were practically giving it away! And we can run it on red diesel!"

"Adam!" said Robin. "Can you lift me...? Adam!"

Robin had managed to get hold of the seatbelt and had pulled himself upside down, trying to get his feet inside the cab, while Martin tugged insistently on Adam's trousers. Then Owl leant over and picked them both up with his big hairy hands, sitting them beside him on the long black seat, where they played with the horn and each had a turn at pretending to drive. Robin looked over the wheel for his mother, but she had turned, shrugging Adam's hand from her shoulder, and was walking away back up the yard.

Later, when Adam had been round the sheep and had cleared a space for the truck between the haystacks, Owl plugged his electric guitar into the wall next to the piano in the hall. It was his last night with them, so they all lit joss sticks and candles, and even Tara was smoking by the time Adam rolled up his sleeves and hunched himself over the piano keys, thumping his feet against the floorboards and beating out trills and basslines with his calloused fingers.

Tara never took much persuasion to sing. She had a voice which departed from everyday things – as distinct from her normal speech as a bird in the air is distinct from a bird on the ground. She sang songs that would send your thoughts in every direction at once, waving her head so that her long, white-blonde hair fell loose across her face and she had to tuck it back behind her ears. She smiled with her shiny green eyes, her long thin nose making shadows on her cheeks, and Robin began to feel a dizziness coming over him, until the breath seemed to shake in his chest, he forgot the maracas that he and Martin were supposed to have been playing, and he wouldn't have been able to take his eyes away from her, even if he had wanted to.

\* \* \*

Andrew always got closer to the dogs in the winter. It had been the way ever since he could remember. With the snow chewed up and dirty in the yard, blown in through the door, through the windows and the holes in the barn roof, the five of them would curl up together in the corner, among the hay, as far from the door as they could manage. They would share out the coldness, move from the inside to the outside of the huddle, licking one another drowsily. Andrew would smell their wiry, tough, hungry smell, the damp in their coats, smell it on himself and feel comfortable. He'd feel the bones beneath their fur and remember times when they had been outside in the rain, when the dogs' sodden bodies were so much smaller than they seemed when they were dry.

All of this depended, of course, on whether any of them had managed to insinuate their way into the kitchen without being banished straight back out again. You could never really tell with Philip. Sometimes only the dogs got banished, sometimes it was all of them, and other times he said nothing at all, and simply sat there staring at the telly. The dogs liked to act fearless – to be the last to stop chasing a car away down the track, the nearest to sinking their teeth into its insolent foreign tyres – but the truth was that Philip had only to growl and they would be wagging pitifully. He had only to whistle for one of them, and the chosen dog would be preening itself for the rest of the day.

The kitchen had warmth, it had dryness and the promise of leftovers, but above all it had a sense of privilege. In the rare times when a neighbour had been over, the dogs would rove around the kitchen, the toilet, the lounge and the bedroom, cocking their legs on anything polluted by the smell, restoring everything to its natural order. Sometimes they would get so immersed that they would forget all about pursuing the intruder off Philip's property, and the intruder would just drive away with nobody to remind him where he was at all.

The most coveted spot on the whole farm was the space in front of the Rayburn – rarely achieved because Andrew's mother, Dora, was almost always standing there, the steam from her saucepans rising around her and condensing on the tattered wallpaper, with its muddy colours and strangled-looking flowers. Now and then, Andrew found it hard to tell where the Rayburn began and his mother ended. The two of them seemed to blur together, black cloth and black metal, the way that fence posts blur with the sides of trees.

The dogs didn't pay much attention to Dora, except to ensure that they weren't stepped on when she made one of her periodic journeys from the Rayburn to the sink. On one occasion, Vaughn had darted in front of her and had wound up with scalds all down his back. But the dogs learnt to look out for such things – like they learnt not to fall in the cesspit, not to climb onto the table and try to steal food, and not to wander off across the rotten floors and the scattered, broken glass of the abandoned rooms.

Werndunvan was a big old farmhouse, built on a ledge on the side of a hill named Cold Winter. Philip, Dora and Andrew lived in four small rooms on the down-stairs floor, where Philip's parents had lived before them, but above them and through the walls there were rooms where the windows were broken, where plaster had fallen in chunks from the walls and the ceilings and the furni-ture was sinking through the floors. Streams had worked their way down from the cracks and the missing slates in the roof, weaving down the corridors and the staircases, turning the hallways into deltas of lime-coloured dirt.

But there were dry rooms, too, and dry spaces even in the wet rooms, places where you could sit and play among the rubble and the mouldering upholstery. To Andrew these were places of wonder – crowded, as they were, with the wreckage of former inhabitants.

Philip had locked the door in the lounge between their side and the other, even blocked up the cracks at the edges with newspaper, but there was a door at the opposite end of the building which was always open, and Andrew could reach the catch with a stick. He would go through there often, wandering between the rooms, inspecting the pictures on the walls and the old carpets, peering into boxes or simply curled up in a corner, wrapped in a dust-heavy blanket, smelling the smells beneath the farm's competing reeks: the sharpness of the mice and the bats in the roof, the sweetness of the alien plants in the jungle of a garden, the weight of the dampness in the stone and the wood, the essence of decay.

# CHAPTER TWO

# CHRISTMAS

Near the end of the winter term, Mr Gwynne, the new Infants schoolteacher, arranged a stargazing expedition on the hill beyond Offa's Bank. Everyone in the class was invited, but in the end only three children came: Robin, Jessica, the doctor's daughter, and Nigel, whose parents had moved to the village from Cardiff a couple of years earlier. Other parents said that they had quite enough to do already, what with the stock to feed and the nativity play coming up, and a couple of them muttered that old Mrs Crabbit had never had these crackpot ideas.

Mr Gwynne had moved to the village only that summer. He was tall and slim, with dark floppy hair that spilt onto his shoulders and little round glasses that he would turn in his hands when he was thinking. All the girls in the Juniors wished that he was teaching them instead. His family, they soon discovered, came from a town in North

Wales, near a slate quarry where his father and his brother still worked. He had left to go to university in London and had lived there for several years, but his voice was still unmistakably Snowdonian – deep, soft and rolling. Indeed, he was the first person in the village actually to have spoken Welsh in over a century.

"Night eyes," Mr Gwynne explained as he turned off the headlights, parking his car in a gateway on the left-hand side of the lane. "The sooner we get used to it, the better. Now, you're all going to be warm enough, are you? It can get a bit nippy on these clear nights."

Robin, Nigel and Jessica climbed carefully out onto the muddy verge, looking up at the sky, which for once was open in every direction – without a hill, a cloud or even a tree to interrupt it. Ahead of them, past the sign that welcomed you into England, the dark, flexing hills fell away beneath the thin moon, until there was only a plain where patches of orange smeared the air on the distant horizon.

"Okay," said Mr Gwynne. "Who can see Orion?"

"I can!" said Nigel. "Up there! Look!"

"And the Milky Way!" said Jessica, not to be outdone.

"Caer Gwydion," said Mr Gwynne. "That's what they call the Milky Way in Welsh mythology. I don't know if any of you remember, but Gwydion was a famous magician, the son of Dôn..."

"He turned trees into soldiers," said Robin.

"Just so," said Mr Gwynne, sounding pleased. "I'm glad you were listening, Robin. And he was the brother of Arianhod, whom he chased all along the Milky Way!"

The four of them climbed the gate into the nearest field and walked a few paces until the wall beside the road had shrunk back into the ground. They stood in a line, their backs to the lights and the complications of England, watching as the Milky Way fed itself into the Welsh hilltops. Robin was wearing gloves, a jumper and a thick coat, but already he was beginning to feel the cold and it was some moments before he could steady his arms against his chest and focus his binoculars – one eye after the other, as Adam had shown him.

"You're cold, Robin," said Mr Gwynne. "Did you not bring a scarf?"

"I think I left it in your car," Robin admitted.

Mr Gwynne sighed and set off back towards the lane, his clean wellies crunching on the frozen grass.

"Anyone else forgotten anything?" he called over his shoulder.

"It's not actually mine," Robin called back, by way of a defence. "It's Tara's... She wanted me to bring it."

The Milky Way ran straight above their heads, echoing the border from the faint glow of Abberton over Offa's Bank to the rich black emptiness of the Cefns, and Robin soon began to follow it – past the arching moon, past stars that he knew, like Cygnus, the Pleiades, Castor and Pollux – until he came to a particularly bright star which was sitting on the opposite horizon.

"Is that the Dog Star?" he asked, when he heard Mr Gwynne climbing back over the clattering gate.

He lowered his binoculars and glanced towards him. It was odd but, faint through the darkness, he could have sworn that he saw his teacher press Tara's scarf to his face.

"Whereabouts?" asked Mr Gwynne, enthusiastically.

"Over there," said Robin. He waited until he was a bit closer, and then pointed to the north.

"Yeah," said Mr Gwynne. "Sirius. How on earth did you wind up there, Robin?"

"I followed Caer Gwydion," said Robin.

"Of course." Mr Gwynne smiled and handed him the scarf, then he pointed out Sirius to the others. "And do you know, Jessica, why Sirius is so bright?"

Jessica shook her head.

"Well," said Mr Gwynne, and his voice began to rise and fall, as it always did when he was onto a subject that interested him. "For one thing it's very, very big. Okay? It's twice as massive as the Sun. And, for another, it's really quite nearby. It's only about eight and a half light years away."

"What's the most furthest star?" asked Jessica.

"Well," said Mr Gwynne. "The furthest stars that anyone knows about are fifteen thousand million light years away! That's way beyond anything we could see right now, I'm afraid, but... Let's see. Can you all find Polaris?"

"I can!" said Nigel.

"Good, Nigel." Mr Gwynne followed his finger. "That's it. Dead straight above you. Well, if you look from Polaris across to the nearest part of the Milky Way, and you keep going straight, then you'll come to a star which looks a bit smudged..."

"Is it a planet?" asked Robin.

"No. It's a galaxy called Andromeda. It might look a bit small to us, but it is actually made up of hundreds of billions of stars!"

Robin craned backwards, the binoculars clamped to his eyes, trying not to shiver and miss the galaxy, and, while Mr Gwynne was explaining again how to find it, he suddenly came across a star that resembled a bright little cloud.

"That light," said Mr Gwynne, quietly, a few moments later. "That light you're looking at now set out towards us more than two *million* years ago! Two million years ago! That's long before there were any human beings. Two million years ago, there were still woolly mammoths and sabre-toothed tigers. There were giant rivers of ice running all the way from here to the North Pole... Just think, you're looking at something from all those years ago! You're actually looking back in time!"

\* \* \*

There were already several cars in the mangled snow of the car park when Robin, Tara and Martin arrived at the village hall for the nativity play. The village hall was quite a new building, with a shingled roof and walls of overlapping planks which shook whenever somebody slammed a door. Climbing to the ground, Robin could just make out the ranks of metal chairs through the ice-coated windows, the orange heaters hanging from the beams and the various mothers struggling with pieces of set and exotic-looking headgear, stumbling on their unfamiliar heels.

Tara draped Robin's costume carefully over her arm and, taking Martin's hand, led the way towards the big glass doors, her hips swaying and the flares of her trousers swinging round her ankles. Unlike most of the other mothers, Tara always managed to look graceful, whatever she wore. Other mothers would look uncomfortable in their best clothes – like they would have been far happier in overalls and wellies – but heels and sewn-on sequins would always make Tara look more like herself than ever, the same way that make-up would pronounce her eyes and lips.

Inside, a big empty space led away to the stage, where lights were turning green and yellow, blue, red and orange. Pretty much everyone in the village helped out with the school play – mothers and aunts made costumes, fathers and uncles built bulky pieces of set – and the place was swarming with old women carrying Welsh cakes, boys shouting and driving model cars along the walls, and, through the door of the canteen, Robin could see other children too, changing into their costumes among tea urns, cookers and cupboards, while their mothers made last-minute refinements with safety pins, despairing that they would ever get everything done in time.

"Hiya, Tara!" said Mary Cwmithel, who was crossing the stage beneath a donkey costume. "Alright, boys? Dad not with you?"

"Oh, you know Adam, Mary." Tara smiled and rolled her eyes. "Always something to get finished up first!"

Robin saw Mr Gwynne almost as soon as they arrived in the canteen – sitting on a bench near the back of the room, surrounded by groups of grown-ups and children, his knees beneath a glittering backdrop, which he seemed to be trying to stitch together.

"Noswaith ddu, Mr Gwynne!" said Robin, keenly. "My costume's got a galaxy on it!"

"Excellent, Robin!" Mr Gwynne removed his reading glasses. "And how are your lines getting on?"

"I know Robin's lines!" said Martin.

"I bet you do, Martin!" said Mr Gwynne, shuffling aside to make room on the bench.

Tara hung up her coat and sat down.

"God, Huw," she said, inspecting the backdrop. "What on earth happened to this?"

"Ah..." he laughed, and spread the material across her knees as well. "There's been unrest among the angels."

Robin took his costume carefully from its bin-liner, murmuring his lines nervously beneath his breath. The costume was a rich, deep scarlet – covered in planets and stars, comets and meteors – and it flowed most impressively behind him when he walked. These were the robes of the one Wise Man of the West: an ancient Welsh astronomer who had travelled to the Holy Land along the Milky Way, searching for clearer skies, carrying an early telescope and working on the phenomenon of moving stars.

There was only one Wise Man of the West because there were only twenty children in the whole school, and once you had accounted for Mary and Joseph, Herod, the innkeeper, angels, shepherds, cattle, sheep, both ends of the donkey and Three Wise Men of the East, there weren't a lot of them left. In the Infants' class there was only one other child of Robin's age, Nigel, but he was a whole head taller, and tended to associate with the big boys in the Juniors as much as possible. Still, the two of them did share a passion for astronomy, and they would sit together during lessons, finding out from their charts what time Venus was rising, or building a giant spaceship out of cardboard and tinfoil.

"Did you see *The A-Team* last night?" Nigel asked Robin, as his mother made adjustments to his crown. "When Murdock jumped his car through the middle of that lorry!"

"Yeah! I loved that bit!" Robin lied. He was rarely, if ever, allowed to watch television. "It was like, kapow!" He threw up his hands and pretended to fly backwards through the air.

"And then when it exploded!" said Nigel.

Robin glanced across the room, to check that his mother wasn't listening. But Tara had taken over work on the backdrop – deep in conversation with Mr Gwynne, their heads close together – and, even though he watched them both for several moments, resplendent in his costume, his lines churning and mingling in his head, neither of them looked back at him once.

\* \* \*

Christmas Day was Tara's birthday – as it had once been the birthday of Isaac Newton and Dorothy Wordsworth. It had snowed for most of the previous week and on Christmas Eve, Adam had been forced to use the new truck to get down the track to the main road, so that they could go and buy her presents in Abberton. Robin and Martin had stood waiting in the open field at the bottom of the track's initial slope, wrapped in duffel coats and woolly hats, their gloves joined across the shoulders by pieces of string. The drifts between the hedges had been so high that the truck would vanish for seconds at a time with only the roar of its five-litre engine and the snow exploding behind it to reveal that it was in there at all.

After lunch – segregated as ever between meat and Tara's vegan alternative – they presented Tara with hand-kerchiefs and a new woolly hat, then the four of them went out to the big shed that Adam had built off the edge of the old hay barns. The valley was temporarily calm, the snow settled, and the sky low and cheerless. From the barn, you could look right down into the village – its clusters of tiny stone houses divided up by white fields, the smoke rising straight from their chimneys – the bare English hills beyond them, and the Stone House on the horizon where, so Mr Gwynne said, the famous poet William Wordsworth had once been caught by a thunder-storm and been forced to spend the night.

Beside the shed door, the top of a giant rock pro-truded from the snowy ground – the visible part as long as the kitchen table. While the shed was being built, they had attempted to unearth it, dug down and around it until there was an immense pit into which the rock went down and down. It was one of Robin's earliest memories. The sides of the rock had been covered in tiny scratches, which Adam had explained were made by glaciers during the Ice Age, hundreds of thousands of years ago. But somewhere along the line Robin had begun to confuse it with a meteorite, and convinced himself that the scratches had in fact been caused by tiny meteors on its way through the asteroid belt, heading inexorably for their farm.

Just inside the door, there was a toboggan leaning against the wall, sleek and glistening with linseed oil. It had a length of rope attached in a loop to its front, and its runners were steam-curved, coated with metal and wax.

"Wow!" said Robin.

"Wow!" Martin echoed, reaching to touch it.

Tara, Robin and Martin took their seats on the sledge in order of size, and Adam attached the rope to the back of the Fordson Major tractor, warming his bare hands briefly on the chimney before he climbed onto the fertiliser sacks that cushioned the rusting seat. They slid slowly out of the yard, around the house and down the hill into their small offshoot of the valley, the dogs trotting happily in the ruts behind them.

The farm was a bowl shape set back into the larger hillside: steep fields gathered around a bog which became a sequence of ponds, surrounded by woodland, each with a small waterfall at its lower end when the water was high enough. They lurched across the frozen fields, trailed by sheep, and began to climb the slope of Cold Winter on the other side, Adam lifting the loader to put weight back onto the drive wheels.

He stopped at the boundary with Werndunvan – the top of the longest uninterrupted slope on the farm, where an audience of sheep had converged noisily to meet them. For the most part, the boundary fence ran along the crest of the hill, although one of Werndunvan's fields did spill over onto their side – cut in half by an old track lined with hawthorns, the link between the two farms – meeting their own land only a hundred yards from the back of the house, where the ruins of a tiny cottage were pressed against the hedgerow.

"No!" Tara insisted, shaking her head and laughing. "Birthday privilege! Nothing is going to get me sliding down that hill today... I'm thirty-one, for God's sake! I'm much too old!"

"Ta-ra!" Robin and Martin chorused, but she leant obdurately back against a fence post, and looked away at Offa's Bank as if she'd suddenly seen something there of terrific importance.

"Okay," said Adam. He sat down on the toboggan behind the boys and locked his arms round their shoulders, his breath warm and rich-smelling, making clouds between them. "Here's what you do, okay? If you want to go left, then you dig in your left boot, and if you want to go right, then you dig in your right boot... Got it?"

The snow flew up so fast that Robin could barely see. The dogs were barking and spinning through the snow beside them. The world was passing at a horrendous speed, the hedge at the bottom accelerating towards them. For a moment he remembered asteroids, the excitement rising in a wave in his chest till he thought that they might burn up. Then they hit a lump of some kind and all three of them were rolling over together, whooping and screaming, the dogs hovering beside them now, unsure if this was a game or a terrible accident.

Face-down in the snow, Robin was laughing so hard he could scarcely breathe. Once or twice he tried to roll over, but he only managed to move again when he heard Adam cackling and a snowball burst on the back of his head. At once, he scrambled back to his feet and launched himself towards him, wrapping his arms round his waist while Martin grabbed one of his legs, trying to sweep it out from underneath him. Adam stumbled, waving his arms as if they really were going to be able to knock him over, but then he swept them squirming onto his shoulder and set off back towards the toboggan.

"Come on!" he said. "Let's have another go!"

"Yeah!" said Robin.

"Another go!" said Martin.

He dropped them back in a heap on the toboggan and, frowning slightly at the sound of a tractor, wrapped the string round his hand.

The sound of the tractor grew steadily as Adam dragged the two boys back up the hill, and, by the time they reached the top, there was a tutty red Massey Ferguson on the far side of the fence, all four of the Werndunvan dogs sniffing through the wire at the two sleeker dogs from Penllan, while the sheep of both farms watched from a wary distance. Philip Tolland was pacing out a circle in his field, his eyes pinned to the ground, muttering something incomprehensible to Tara.

"Adam," he nodded, pausing and looking up.

"Philip," said Adam, dropping the string of the toboggan, adopting the Radnorshire slur that he always used with other farmers.

Philip nodded a few times, and adjusted his cap. He wore the same clothes, irrespective of the season – a threadbare jacket over a brown sleeveless jumper, grubby black braces holding up his trousers – and his smell was noxious even at several paces.

"What you got there, boys?" he asked.

"It's a toboggan," Robin murmured, skidding his boot in the snow. "Adam made it for us."

"Beauty, innee!" said Philip.

Behind one of the tyres of the Massey Ferguson, Robin noticed a slight movement: a small dirty face peered out and vanished again, eyes gaping, with a flat cap, a worn old jacket with the sleeves cut short, coming down nearly as far as his knees.

"Hello, Andrew!" said Tara.

"Tara?" said Martin, rubbing his head against her thigh. "Tara, I want another go on the 'boggan!"

"Hang on a minute..." Tara's accent never changed a bit, under any circumstances. "Aren't you going to say Happy Christmas to Philip and Andrew?"

"Happy Christmas, Philip!" said Martin, still half-concealed behind her. "Happy Christmas, Andrew!"

"Happy Christmas!" said Robin a moment later, staring at the pair of enormous boots beneath the tractor.

"And you will send my best to Dora from us, won't you, Philip?" said Tara.

"Right you are," said Philip.

"Please, Tara!" said Martin.

"Well, why not, then?" she agreed, crouching behind Robin and Martin as they climbed back into their places, looping the string over their heads. "So long as we miss that molehill!"

\* \* \*

"How old is Andrew?" asked Robin that evening, once their mother had finished reading to them.

He and Martin were sitting on the arms of an armchair, to either side of her, the hoods pulled up on their green and red dressing-gowns. The living-room was lighter than the drawing-room, with two sets of windows instead of one, fragrant plants on the windowsills, toys, tapes, a telephone and other signs of livingness scattered about the place. The book that Tara had been reading from lay open on her lap – an illustration showed a thin, bedraggled knight in rusty armour clambering from a ditch with his broken lance in one hand.

"Andrew must be almost seven," she said, after a moment's thought. "He's just a few months younger than you, Robin."

"I'm four," protested Martin.

"You're an idiot," said Robin.

"No, I'm not!"

Unusually, Tara paid no attention to their squabbling, stroking her chin with her finger, and instead she seemed to be inspecting the wall across the room. In the hall, Adam was picking out a few chords on the piano – a song by John Lennon, who had recently died – and the smell of his pipe tobacco wafted through the intervening door.

"Why doesn't Andrew go to school, then?" asked Robin.

"Why don't I go to school?" said Martin. "It's not fair!"

"You will go to school soon, Mart." Tara put a hand on his hair. "And Andrew ought to go to school. I'm sure that he'll go there soon enough."

There was a series of high, rippling notes on the piano, then the clack of the lid, and a moment later Adam's head appeared around the doorframe, the pipe in his mouth and his hair standing upright at the front.

"Good story?" he asked.

"There was a knight," said Martin. "And he was riding on his horse, and he went riding right into a branch of a tree and he fell off and he landed in the ditch!"

"Was he okay?" asked Adam, with concern.

"Yes," said Robin. "But his armour was all bent and then his horse went riding off without him!"

"Well!" said Adam, lifting his eyebrows. "And do you think it's your bedtime now, or do you think we ought to go and watch the telly for a few minutes?"

Robin stared at him. Then he turned to Tara to check that this wasn't some kind of joke.

"Oh, go on, then," she said, closing the book. "Seeing as it's Christmas. But only for a bit. Then you are both coming upstairs for a bath."

The two boys scurried through the hall into the drawing-room and Robin jumped over the back of the sofa, rolling on top of the cushions. Going to the corner, Adam unlocked the cupboard and fiddled with the dial on the television until the air was filled with strange, high noises.

A series of white dots moved across the black-and-white screen, then a tall dark man in a suit and a bowler hat came striding into a circle, turned and fired a gun straight towards them. A moment later, there were the shapes of dancing women, rising strings and the twang of an electric guitar, and, curled next to Adam, who for once smelt of whisky and tobacco instead of sheep, Robin watched almost without breathing – jumping when a man got shot in the back, and when a car came screeching from a shadowy side-street and carried the murderers away.

Across the room, Tara sat in the armchair near the woodburner, writing in her diary, as she did every night. From time to time, she looked over at the three of them – Adam jiggling his legs when things got exciting, Martin perched on his lap, Robin goggling from the cushions and the folds of his dressing-gown – and she watched for a few moments before she returned her attention to the page.

Later, when Tara had dozed off, the tall dark man was in a jungle full of waterfalls with a beautiful blonde woman in a white bikini, and when the woman declared that there was a real, fire-breathing dragon nearby Robin thought that nothing in the world could have got any better. He loved dragons, and especially the battling red and white dragons that Mr Gwynne had told them about at school, that King Lludd had captured by digging a hole in the precise centre of Britain and lowering in a cauldron of mead to make them drowsy.

King Lludd had moved them to Snowdonia, of course, where he'd buried them in a kistvaen, and where, five hundred years later, the evil King Vortigern had tried to build a tower, which invariably fell down during the night. It was the boy Merlin who had revealed the truth, digging beneath the tower to uncover the dragons who, by night, were fighting each other still: the cowardly white dragon of the Saxon invaders and the brave red dragon of the Celts.

\* \* \*

Beneath the kitchen table at Werndunvan, Andrew and Meg were playing with a ball that had materialised from somewhere earlier that evening: red, pink and white, carved with the smiling face of an old man with a beard. The two of them fought for it, wrestling and feigning anger, occasionally darting out across the floor to catch it before they darted back behind the blue plastic curtains of the tablecloth, where you could pretty well believe that you were invisible, where no one else could possibly ever know that you were there.

Outside of the tablecloth, a couple of the dogs were dozing among the scattered chairs, gnawed bones and bits of shredded newspaper that covered the floor – as near to the Rayburn as possible without getting under Dora's unpredictable feet. As usual, she was in the coveted spot, rocking gently over the bar, the front of her black dress lifted slightly by her stomach, her thin dark hair tangled with grey, cut vaguely to her shoulders. Four or five plumes of steam were rising around her. The droplets that formed on the ceiling converged into drops, which hung more and more heavily until they splashed back down to the floor in splotches of cleanliness.

Outside of the kitchen, the night was clear and far below zero. The stars seemed hardly higher than the chimneys, shining from the fat waves of snow spread across the hills, while the smudges of woodland looked more like holes in the earth than anything substantial. Only the one window of the house was alight – small, dirty and all but buried in the hillside. The front gate seemed open in welcome, not because its hinges were snapped and the earth and grass had moulded themselves around its lower bars. A foot of snow hid the broken slates and the corrugated iron that clung to the roof. The glass in the windows shone in independent constellations.

With a rush of freezing air, Philip reappeared with Vaughn in the kitchen door, kicking off the snow on the doorstep and his boots on the lino, padding across the floor in poorly darned socks till he reached the shelf where he kept his GI cider. Taking one of the brown litre bottles and the glass that he always used, he sat down at the table, pushed his feet towards the Rayburn, tipped back his cap on his head and filled himself a pipe.

On the television, James Bond had finally been trapped, his sidekick killed and the dragon revealed as a tank with a flame-thrower on the front – not that Andrew, Philip or Dora was paying it much attention.

"Buggerin' hell, but it's cold!" said Philip contentedly, through the smoke. "What's for tea, missus?"

Dora's rocking steadied a little and she began to shuffle the pans around on the hotplates.

"Lamb," she muttered, stirring something furiously.

Vaughn cocked his leg against the sideboard and Philip swore at him, inspecting the couple of cards they'd received from the neighbours: the usual mix-up of reindeer with fluorescent noses, mistletoe and small blond children with wings. Naturally, they hadn't sent any cards themselves. Under the table, Andrew and Meg remained motionless, the ball still on the floor behind them, Philip's face discernible through the crack in the tablecloth that followed the crease on the corner.

"I'm going to build a fucking good shed, I am," remarked Philip, his eyes on Ursula Andress while Dora stumped across the room with a saucepan, steam billowing out behind her. "We need a shed and that's just the bloody place for him. On the flat behind the barn, there! Perfect!"

Dora returned to the Rayburn with a leg of lamb and poured sauce onto it from a second pan before she deposited it on the table. The meat had been boiled till it had mostly come loose from the bone. The sauce, on inspection, was custard. Philip clasped his fork and moved several large lumps to his mouth. Then he drained his glass and filled it back up again.

Leaning back in his chair, he lifted up the edge of the tablecloth and peered beneath it, frowning.

"You under there, boy?" he said. Then, seeing that he was, he removed a piece of the lamb with his fingers, dunked it in the custard and tossed it down to him.

"Here you are, girl," he told Meg, as he threw her down a piece of her own.

# CHAPTER THREE

# A NEW FOCUS

In February, the snow turned to rain, dissolving the ice on the grass of the open fields and filling the streams again so the intricate ice constructions that spanned the banks or stretched between rocks were smashed and sucked away. The rain ate into the snowdrifts in the valleys, driving them back into the hills and shaded places, until by the end of the month the only snow left was in the quarries on Cold Winter where the sheep sheltered, and in the gritty remains of an immense heap that Adam had built behind the house with the Fordson Major. This – to Robin, at least – came finally to resemble Criccieth Castle, which he had learnt about at school: the great thirteenth-century stronghold of Llywelyn ap Iorwerth, the famous towers of its gatehouse jutting on its headland into the clear blue water of Tremadoc Bay.

\* \* \*

At Werndunvan, a week or two before lambing, Meg gave birth to four puppies in the loose hay beneath the haystack – squirming and squeaking, swatting one another with their frog-like legs and dragging themselves blindly towards her leaking teats. Suddenly, the world had a new focus. Vaughn paced around them, eyeing the nest, the balls of black-and-white fluff, sniffing at the raw, new smell and not at all sure what to make of it. Occasionally, when the puppies were asleep, Meg stretched and wandered out into the rain, her teats flopping beneath her. But she never went further than the edges of the yard, never pursued a departing car, ignored the postman as he deposited the letters in the box on the gatepost.

It wasn't so much that Meg's character had changed, more that she seemed to be operating under instructions from somewhere else. The instructions told her to eat the gore in the hay behind her, to lie on her side, to lick these little creatures clean as she licked herself, to attempt to keep them warm. Initially, she had been just as surprised by it all as Andrew was, but soon enough it was as normal to her as anything else and the look of astonishment faded from her face.

The nest was in a corner against the draughty back wall of the barn, and the wind sang as it came through the holes. Andrew sat beside her for much of the first day, watching her, watching the reactions of the other dogs, until, as night began to come on and his eyes peered deeper into the darkness, he felt instructions of his own rising up in him and lay down with his back against the wall, sheltering the puppies from the rain running in between the weatherboards, wrapping himself firmly in the hay.

Peculiar thoughts came to him sometimes, whilst he was lying there, stroking Meg's throat, talking in whines or singing her tunes from the telly. Instead of things that were, he'd think of things that could be. He'd look at the puppies, or smell them if it was night-time – their raw smell thickening with shit and piss, milk and saliva – and then he'd think about an animal who might come to hurt them: its teeth, its claws, its eyes yellow with cruel thoughts. But, instead of simply feeling fear, the back of his head would start to prickle, his lips would twitch and pull away from his teeth. He would even try to wish this animal into existence, just so he could destroy it, just so he could tear it to shreds in their defence.

\* \* \*

The morning after the Frickers arrived, the entire house at Penllan smelt of old cigarette smoke, and the kitchen table was covered in empty wine bottles, scrunched-up cigarette packets, beer cans and ashtrays which had flooded in every direction. A series of big muddy footprints trailed across the red tile floor from the boot-passage, circled among the scattered chairs and headed back out again, and on the sideboard there was a funny little man whose matchstick legs were buried in a dollop of wax, his bright-orange face grinning from a fat cork body.

"Who made the little man, Tara?" asked Robin.

"Can I play with him, Tara?" said Martin. "Tara!"

But Tara said nothing as she brought them their wheat flakes – the two of them perched side by side on the bench, beginning to wonder what had happened – and she returned to the washing-up in such a way that the sink, the plates and the water might all have evaporated and she would probably have gone on making all of the same movements irrespective. She was wearing a strange, long, hairy coat that Robin had never seen before and staring out of the window at the ridge of Cold Winter above the bare, brown larch wood, where the two boys would sometimes point out a dinosaur with a long neck, nodding continually, although Tara had always seemed unable to see it.

Layla Fricker was Tara's best friend from when she was at school – long before Robin and Martin were born, long before Tara and Adam had even met. Together they had gone on family holidays to the Côte d'Azur, almost been expelled and grown their hair until they could sit on it. They had been all the way to India on the back of a lorry with a group of German musicians, had played concerts in the desert there, learnt how to eat fire, and danced around with long, swirling bits of cloth. Some of these were still in the cupboard under the stairs, and Tara would drag them out from time to time, when they were having a party.

The Frickers shared a large, half-timbered farmhouse in Llanddewi-Brefi with a pair of other families whose names Robin didn't know. So Klaus and Cloud, the Fricker children, lived with lots of other boys and girls, who were a bit like their brothers and sisters. Layla and Mike and the other parents had a special room in the barns across the yard that they used as a classroom, and they all took turns as teachers because they didn't like the local school. They had three huge tepees in the garden and a vegetable patch so big that it supplied them all the whole year round. But Adam had once said that the only reason any of them had moved to Llanddewi-Brefi in the first place was because it had a pretty name.

"Tara?" said Robin finally, unable to bear the silence any longer. "Can we get down now? Please?"

Tara started and turned round. She went to arrange her hair, noticed that she was still wearing her rubber gloves and peeled them off.

"Yes," she said. "Sorry, boys. Yes, of course... Sorry, I was miles away. We had a bit of a late night last night, I'm afraid."

"Aren't Klaus and Cloud awake yet?" asked Robin.

"No," said Tara. "No, I think they're still asleep."

"Tara?" said Martin.

"Can I show them the ponds later on?" asked Robin.

"Yes, I expect so."

"Can we go up Cold Winter?"

"Tara? Why are you wearing that funny coat?"

"Look," said Tara. She looked so exhausted suddenly that both Robin and Martin fell instantly silent, terrified that she might shout at them. "I've got a lot of things to do in here, okay? So why don't the two of you go outside and play for a bit? Okay? Go and play with the skulls or something."

* * *

A few weeks earlier, Martin had found a sheep skull. At the time the boys and Tara were on the way to see Mrs Hughes – a very old lady who lived with her son Bill Llanoley across the valley, and who had recently taken to inviting Tara around every time that Bill left the farm. The skull was in a state of some decomposition, and something had been gnawing on it, but Martin became attached to it immediately and carried it all the way back to the farm, where he sat it on the wall beside the woodshed.

Over the following days, he located half a dozen other sheep skulls, as well as two intact chicken skulls, which the cats had been picking at in the straw on the floor of the barn. Then, while he and Robin were making dens in the hayloft, pushing over stacks of bales, they came across an entire nest of kittens, abandoned by the mother and containing seven complete skeletons with bits of skin and fur still clinging onto them. These Robin was all for leaving well alone, but Martin insisted on gathering them up, and arranged them in a group beside the skulls – the bank in front of them thick with snowdrops and the swollen yellow heads of daffodils.

A minute or two after the boys arrived outside, Adam appeared in the field below the larch wood, his cap pulled down firmly against the wind. The slope was gradual, so it was a few moments before they could see his whole face – his cheeks pale with stubble and the lines prominent around his eyes – then his tattered coat, his mud-spattered jeans and wellies and, finally, the dogs, who were padding along behind him, their eyes on the ground and their expressions distinctly nervous.

"Your mother inside?" Adam grunted, as he opened the gate. The two of them nodded and greeted the dogs, fussing over them while Adam approached the kitchen window, one of his wellies sucking wetly on his foot, cupping his hands against the reflections of the trees and the sky.

"Tara?" he said. "Could you help me a moment, please?"

"What's happened?" she asked.

"The Fordson's in the fucking bog," he said. "I'll need you to drive the other tractor."

Tara sighed and lifted a sheet from the sink, twisting it so that water poured from the middle. She plumped it on the draining board and pulled her rubber gloves off again, rolling down the sleeves of her long, peculiar coat, which, from where Robin was standing, made her seem fuzzy round the edges.

"Those friends of yours up yet?" he said.

"It's a Saturday morning," said Tara. "What the fuck do you think?"

\* \* \*

The Fordson Major had been on the farm since the Second World War. It was big and tough as an old dog, with none of the modern tractor fripperies like cabs or speedometers to complicate matters. It had a pulley on the side which you could connect to a saw or a swede-crusher, red wheels, blue bodywork, and headlights which stuck out from either side of its radiator like a pair of protruding eyes.

When Robin, Tara and Martin arrived among the winter-brown rushes at the edge of the bog, the Fordson's back wheels were sunk most of the way to the axles in the sodden ground and its nose was lurching upwards like it was gasping for air. Adam stopped the smaller tractor – an old Ferguson – half a dozen yards from the Fordson, flipped away the throttle lever and fastened a chain to its back. Tara towed the heavy chain to the front of the Fordson, looking no more cheerful than she had done in the kitchen, then she removed her coat and hung it on the nearest hazel, where it swayed and fluttered among the catkins.

So far as Robin was aware, Adam had never got a tractor stuck before in his life. Adam was such a good driver that people from as far away as Crug and Bleddfa had phoned him to help them extract their machine from a pond, or to remove it from the edge of a dingle, where it was trapped in such a way that all four of its wheels were isolated from the ground.

"The ground's completely waterlogged," said Adam, as they conferred in the space between the two tractors. "If you could just take up the slack as gently as you can? I'll disconnect the feeder... It's worth a shot. You never know."

"Stand right back, boys," Tara called. "If the chain comes loose or anything, it can be very, very dangerous." She twisted her hair up into a bun, pinning it in place with a pencil. "Okay?"

The two of them stood on adjacent tufts of reeds about halfway across the bog, Martin sucking his thumb, watching as the chain began to lift from the ground. Tara was looking over her shoulder, her eyes on the chain, her right hand working the throttle. Behind her, Adam was hunched on his cushion of fertiliser bags – his posture precisely as it was when he was playing the piano – his eyes shifting from the Fordson's few instruments to the wheels beneath him, to the chain, to the Ferguson, his hands on the throttle lever and the steering wheel, his feet hovering beside the brakes and the clutch.

As the chain began to pull, the Fordson surged against the bank in front of it, roared, poured smoke from its chimney, rolled back and surged forwards again, an arc of mud spitting into the air behind it. For a moment, it was working so furiously that it seemed it would have to escape, but then Adam was signalling with his hand, falling back in his seat, and Tara reversed slowly until the chain was lying back on the ground.

"Adam!" she was saying as the boys came running up. "For Christ's sake! We went over all this last night! Layla and Mike are leaving this afternoon! We were going to take this one morning off!"

"I'm sorry, Tara," Adam shrugged. "What can I do? I mean, we can't leave the damn thing here, can we?"

✳ ✳ ✳

Left to themselves for half an hour, Robin and Martin discovered that the various pools and puddles in the bog were at different levels, and that with some careful footwork it was possible to channel one into another. They built an impressive, semicircular dam between a pair of tussocks, then flooded an entire ocean behind it, complete with islands and cliffs, treacherous sandbanks and ports full of steep, winding streets and gloomy inns where pirates sat around plotting and brave young boys were abducted into lives at sea. They had just launched a pair of sticks by way of ships when they heard the sputter of another tractor in the field behind them and Bill Llanoley arrived in the gateway, stopping to greet Adam and Tara.

Bill was by far their friendliest neighbour. He talked to everyone with exactly the same wide-open grin, expos-ing teeth that were either smashed, black or missing altogether. The day that Tara returned from the hospital with Martin, he had been up on Offa's Bank, looking for a missing ewe. He had walked nearly five miles to see the baby, giving them a four-leaved clover that he found on the way, before turning around and walking all the way back again.

"That's a hell of a hole you got him in there, boys," said Bill, grinning at Robin and Martin. "Much deeper, and that's the last you'll see of the old Fordson!"

The dogs were smelling one another's bottoms.

"The ground's completely waterlogged," said Robin.

"Weather's been bloody murder," Bill agreed, shaking his head. "Mother's sitting in a puddle in the kitchen at home, and she's none too pleased about it, I'll tell you that much!"

Martin giggled and Bill grinned back, revealing a mangled wisdom tooth, then he hoisted his trousers up through the baler twine round his waist, and set about connecting his John Deere to the front of the Ferguson.

By the time that the Frickers arrived, the Fordson had sunk as far as its back axle, and both the Ferguson and the John Deere were chained into a line – spattered with mud and stuck inextricably. On the downwind side of the John Deere, Bill and Adam were puffing on their pipes, trying to work out what to do next through the rumble of the engines and the clatter of the chimney-caps.

"You just got to put up with Philip Tolland," Bill was saying, thoughtfully. "I tell you... We used to be mates when we was kids, and he was a miserly devil back then and all. Mother was mates with old Mrs Tolland, look. They was mates right up to the time she died, and that must have been ten years ago if it's a day."

"They say it was a tidy place, Werndunvan," said Adam. "Once upon a time."

"Once upon a time, ar," Bill nodded. "When I was a kid, old Robert was still running things. They was still living in them same four rooms, but he ment all the holes in the hedges, and he'd got some lovely stock over there, he had. Got some Friesians. Got some 'erefords..." He whistled, shaking his head. "But even with the old girl scrattin' on, there was still only me and John the Glyn who was talking to him, that's how much he'd pissed us all off! Philip wouldn't marry till his mother had gone, look! Didn't care how old Dora got... Wouldn't give her the bloody pleasure!"

In appearance, Bill and the Frickers could hardly have been more different. They could easily have belonged to different species. Where Bill wore a mud-grey jacket with matching boots and trousers, Mike had on a diaphanous shirt and velvet bell-bottoms – both in brilliant colours, regardless of whether he was about to get mud all over them – while Layla wore a bright red dress that reached the whole way down to the ground. Where Bill had short, neatly cropped hair beneath his cap, all of the Frickers had dark hair falling past their shoulders – and Layla and Cloud could both conceal their bottoms completely. They also had entire mouthfuls of teeth.

"Do you want to see our ocean?" Martin asked Klaus and Cloud, as the two groups met.

"What ocean?" said Klaus.

"The ocean we're building..." Martin started.

"Let's go and see the hollow tree!" said Robin, quickly. "There's a hollow tree in the wood past the ponds, and you can get right into its middle!"

Klaus was a good couple of years older than Robin and several times more knowledgeable. Like his sister Cloud, he looked at the tractors in a way that suggested that he could have resolved the problem in a moment, if only someone had thought to ask him. He had an earring without looking like a girl, and because Layla was half-Egyptian he had a kind of piratical look about him, which Robin found both admirable and mysterious.

Sitting on the chain between the Ferguson and the Fordson, Tara and Layla were swinging and balancing with their arms. They were looking at their feet, talking in a thoughtful kind of way, and Tara seemed a good deal more relaxed than she had been over breakfast.

"I don't know, Layl," she was saying. She was wearing her hairy coat again. "I do still write the odd poem in my diary. But... I like to have something that's just for me, do you know what I mean? Especially when everything's public property, the way it is round here."

"But they're good!" Layla insisted. "You know they are! I mean, I could recite a couple of them just off the top of my head. They're really vivid, you know... They've got a real sense of life."

"Tara?" Robin asked nervously. "Can we go and see the hollow tree, please?"

"Oh, Robbo," said Tara. "Can't you see I'm busy?"

"Doing what?" said Robin.

"Tara?" said Martin. "I've got water in my welly."

"Tara!" called Adam above the noise of the tractors. "Me and Bill are going to have to go round Werndunvan, I'm afraid. See if we can't get Philip over with that new tractor of his."

Rain was spreading up the valley from the south – hissing in the hedgerows, throwing a pall across the house and the fields around it. At first, the circles were isolated in the pools of the bog, their little waves spreading away down the channels and the inlets of Robin and Martin's miniature ocean. But then it was raining harder and the circles began to overlap, becoming teeming patterns, the raindrops leaping upwards from the surface as they fell, falling again to leave a second perfect ring inside the first.

"Well," Tara swung Martin up onto her hip, removing his boot and emptying it into the grass. She sighed and turned to Adam. "It looks like I'm going to have to go and change Martin's socks anyway, so I suppose I'd better come back up with you."

\* \* \*

Philip's red Mercedes tractor turned off the track from Werndunvan just as the rain was beginning to ease. You could see the hawthorns clearly now on the hard, bare hillside and the huge machine rose up through a space between the trees and plunged down the slope with total confidence, a couple of dogs as outriders, running just to remain alongside.

Robin started running himself when he saw it, as did Klaus, Cloud and Martin, leaving the wood where they had been discussing the idea of a tree house with a drawbridge. They jumped the puddles of the bog, leaping from grass to reeds, moving so fast that it was impossible to think more than a step in front of them, mud spurting up from their wellies, following the strange, winding paths that the solid ground happened to present.

Adam was opening the gate into the bog-field when Robin, Cloud and Klaus arrived breathlessly beside him and the Mercedes made its grand entrance: the biggest talking point at school for the past week, the only tractor of its kind in the whole of Wales. It was twice the size of Adam's blue truck, with no trace of rust on the whole of its body, and all four of its wheels were bigger and fatter than even the back wheels of the Fordson Major.

"Cool!" said Cloud.

Philip descended the steps with all the pomp of a king. He looked across the crowd at Bill and Adam, at Mike leaning against the Ferguson with his drooping black moustache and a long, thin cigarette hanging from his lips, at Tara, Layla and their gawping children, and for a moment he seemed to be about to make a speech. But there was little you could add to such a tractor that it didn't say already – the great black bars across its radiator, the two-inch tread of the tyres, the scowling expression of the headlights – and Philip contented himself with a few grunts and nods.

"Adam," he muttered. "Bill." He surveyed the line of chained-up tractors. "Bit of a spot you got yourselves into here, eh?"

"Ar," Adam nodded, his hands pushed firmly into the pockets of his jeans. "It is that. Good of you to come over, Philip. We were running out of ideas, I don't mind telling you."

"Well, here's a few ideas for you, anyhow!" Philip chuckled, patting a giant tyre. "Six cylinder turbo, four-wheel drive... Only come over from Germany last fucking week, she did!"

He took his pipe from the pocket of his jacket, packed it with tobacco from a ragged-looking pouch and lit it with a few brisk puffs. Coughing thickly, he walked round to the back of the tractor, cursing the sheepdogs milling beneath his feet, and began to root through the fencing

wire, hay bales, sledgehammers, sheep-lick and old fertiliser bags that he had already managed to assemble. He
came back carrying a chain of huge proportions and pro-
pelling Andrew out onto the open grass, where he stood
frozen for a moment, staring wildly at the waves of faces
in front of him.

Up until a year earlier, Robin had been subject to
seizures whenever he was startled. If a car horn went off
unexpectedly, someone broke a plate or even knocked
on the door, he would go rigid, his eyes would roll back
into his head and he would wet himself and collapse.
Afterwards, he could never remember anything about it,
which sometimes made him think that it hadn't really
happened at all, but when he saw the look in Andrew's
eyes he remembered suddenly the sick, empty terror that
had preceded the feeling of dizziness. It made him think
of a night when someone had turned off the light on
the landing and he had thought that he was blind, of a
day when they had been to Jim Garraway's down in the
village, where the sheep had been waiting for slaughter
– knowing their own deaths from the smells of fear and
blood coming from the door in front of them.

"Who is that?" hissed Cloud.

"Andrew," said Robin, faintly.

"He looks like an animal!" said Cloud.

"He looks like he stinks!" Klaus added.

Andrew had dirt smeared on his face, his flat cap spilt
backwards onto his shoulders, his huge jacket flapped
around his knees and his head was twisted down and
to the right, as if he was peering into his armpit. Several

yards away, Tara was sitting on the chain, but she stood up almost as soon as Andrew appeared, moving carefully among the puddles until she could almost have reached out and touched him – when she stopped and crouched down slowly, smiling, talking in a voice that was lost in the thunder of the tractors.

Beyond them, Philip had climbed back up into the cab of the Mercedes and was turning it around, joining the end of the line, where Adam and Bill attached the chain to the John Deere. As Adam paced around the Fordson, kicking mud from the encrusted tyres, Tara allowed one of her hands to hang forward, invitingly, and by the time that Robin looked back at them she was holding Andrew's hand, walking him towards the patch of dry ground where he and the three other children were standing in an awkward cluster.

"Andrew," said Tara, as they arrived. "This is Klaus and this is Cloud..."

Klaus looked wary, one hand fiddling with the collar of his velvet jacket, while Cloud sucked a bunch of her hair, kneading a rag which she took from the pocket of her rainbow-coloured coat.

"And these are Robin and Martin," Tara continued. She caught Robin's eye, and held it for a moment. "Who you know already... I was thinking that perhaps you could all watch the tractors together. And maybe afterwards you could show Andrew what you've been doing with the puddles, boys?"

"Okay, Tara," said Robin, tortured with embarrassment.

"Good boy," said Tara.

Andrew kept his head in the same, twisted position, but his eyes moved steadily, following Tara as she walked back through the mud and the puddles towards the old grey Ferguson, climbed back up onto the wet metal seat, pressed down the clutch and forced it into gear.

Beside the Mercedes, the other, mud-spattered tractors looked tired, cheap and fragile. The mighty engine blew signals of black smoke from its chimney. Philip, Bill, Tara and Adam swapped signals, and then, with a bellow, the huge treads sank into the ground, the first chain began to lift and, spluttering, the John Deere rolled forwards. At the same time, the chain behind it was tightening and, in turn, the Ferguson was prised out with little more than a lurch. Half-buried in the marshy ground, the Fordson was a more difficult proposition, but its own chain to the Ferguson was pretty much tight already, and the Mercedes continued to move relentlessly forwards. A balloon of oily smoke rose from the chimney, the noise of the engine growing into a roar, and the Fordson popped suddenly from its hole, filthy, its limbs loose and frail like an old man's.

On their patch of dry ground, Klaus and Cloud had moved a little way away now, and were talking to one another too quietly for Robin to hear. From the gaggle of sheepdogs, a collie with a white face and a wolfish look about it came up to Andrew and prodded him firmly in the chest with its nose. His shoulders slumped forwards, his head still pressed towards his armpit, Andrew was peering almost directly into the dog's tawny eyes, and he fell to stroking it at once, murmuring something, check-ing on Tara as she detached the chains from the front and the back of the Ferguson. Unsure what else to do, Robin ran his hands along the dog's back, as did Martin, who was soon scratching the hair behind its ears until it was grumbling with pleasure.

"No!" said Cloud, through the falling noise of the tractors. She put her hands to her mouth. "Not really?!"

"Oh, yes!" said Klaus. "That's a werewolf, alright! I'd know one anywhere!"

\* \* \*

The pond at Werndunvan was at the bottom of the hill, between the fields and the forestry, the big dark hills to the west concealed here by the lines of the pines. It was raining again, but then it was always raining. The only difference was that there was no wind to speak of, so the rain fell straight, flattening the thin grass and running through the holes in Philip's raincoat.

There were, of course, circles on the pond, but Philip barely noticed them. He barely noticed the stench of his clothes, or even the heavy sack in his hands. He had, after all, known only these things for the past fifty years. He didn't need to notice the bloody forestry, or that it was bloody raining again, as it was always bloody raining. On the farm, he knew everything important already. The pond was important because it gave the stock somewhere to drink, because the occasional idiot gave him money to

fish there, because it was a back-up in the extremely unlike-
ly event of the water supply running out. The forestry was
beyond his fence, so it wasn't his concern, except to filch a
few Christmas trees once a year, to make a few quid.

Back up in the yard, the dogs had started barking,
which meant that the man from the Ministry had arrived
to talk about the grant for Philip's new shed – his smart
new shed, with its arching metal roof, its tidy oak weatherboarding keeping out the snow in the winter and the rain
all of the rest of the year.

Philip secured the knot on the top of the sack, ignoring the squirming of the puppies inside, and threw it out
firmly into the rain. He watched the splash, then hunched
his coat up further around his neck. The circle it made
was bigger than the others on the pond's surface, but it
was lost soon enough in the general turmoil.

"One thing we don't need", he mumbled, as he turned
back up the hill towards the yard, "is more fucking dogs."

By the time that he reached the yard, he had forgotten all about the puppies, and his attention was fixed on
the pale green Vauxhall Cavalier parked against the barn,
a couple of the dogs circling it suspiciously, barking in
bursts, while Meg wandered anxiously through the mud
a little way further up the hill, her teats swaying heavily
beneath her. The windows of the car were steamed up,
but Philip could just make out the shape of a man inside,
decanting himself a cup of coffee from a Thermos flask.

The thought crossed Philip's mind of hammering on
the window and seeing if he could get the man to scald
himself, but he quickly thought better of it.

"Ah!" The man scrambled from the car, pulling up the hood of his anorak. "You must be Mr Tolland?"

Philip disliked him instantly, his tie and checked shirt and spotless wellingtons. He was the sort that normally he would expel without even allowing him to speak. But he was determined to keep himself under control today, so he contented himself with the involuntary wince that crossed the man's face when he smelt him and the barns around them.

"Ar," said Philip, scowling through the rain.

"My name's Davies," said the man, and smiled. "Dave Davies."

Philip continued to scowl at him.

"I understand..." said the man, glancing up the yard at Andrew, who was on his hands and feet, worming through the rubbish piled against the barn walls. "I understand that you are interested in planning permission for a new shed... I'm from the Ministry of Agriculture, you see."

"S'right," said Philip, and set off without warning towards the corner of the barn and the yard gate, allowing the man to hurry along behind him.

"That your son there, is it?" said the man, trying to sound friendly.

"Ar," said Philip.

"At the school down in the village, is he?" asked the man. "Nice little place, that. I had a niece there a few years back..."

Philip stopped at the derelict area behind the barns, where there was a long, deep trough cut into the ground for a sheep-dip.

"Well," said the man, managing a smile. "At least there's no doubt where you'd put the shed, eh!"

Philip paused, cold water running down his neck, into the groove of his spine, down into the back of his trousers. He felt a wave of fury that he could scarcely control, and for a second or two it was all he could do not to turn round and throttle the man.

Beyond the barns, through the noise of the pissing rain, he could hear Meg whimpering, the sound growing occasionally into barks – a second voice barking along, which irritated him more than ever.

"No, no," said Philip, squeezing out the words. "This ain't the place here."

"Well... Where then?"

Hearing the incomprehension in the man's voice, Philip felt immediately better, although it didn't solve the problem of where he was now going to put the shed. He looked around him, at the present row of barns facing the house, the small shed at the bottom of the yard, then at the hillside sloping away beneath them towards the pond and the rain-scratched forestry.

"Just down there," he said. "Down on the slope there."

He pointed at the nearest field, with its streaming water and its cowering ewes.

"What do you mean, 'there'?" said the man, now thoroughly baffled. "Surely..."

"No, no," said Philip, warming to the idea. "That's the place for him, on the slope there."

"But that's twenty-five, thirty degrees!" said the man. "You'd have to dig out the whole hillside! You'd need bulldozers, earth-moving equipment, drainage... You'd be cutting into the bedrock!"

"That's the place," repeated Philip belligerently.

Beside him, the Ministry man looked deflated. Behind the barn, Meg and Andrew finally stopped their search for the missing puppies and joined their voices in a long, empty howl. The man produced a small pad of paper and, leaning forward to shield it from the rain, began to make a few notes.

# CHAPTER FOUR

# GROWLING AND WAILING

That day Adam delivered seventeen lambs. Skinny creatures with umbilical cords trailing beneath them, they
pulled themselves up onto trembling legs and stared
around at the great dark shed, the couple of light bulbs
on poles between the hurdles, the hulking figure of Adam
beside them washing yellow slime from his arm in a plastic
bucket. Then – or so you would have had to assume – they
saw a second hulking form and forgot everything else that
they'd just been witness to, subject to a sudden, fantastic
urge to absorb its warmth, to suckle for as long as they
were able to, then to lie down, close their eyes and return
promptly to wherever they'd just come from.

Turning off the tap, Adam rolled the sleeve of his shirt,
then his jumper, back down, shivering in the draught that

came beneath the big doors, between the weatherboards, and out through the old barns behind him. Around him, expectant ewes were gathered in groups, in alleys of pens, stirring and scrunching on hay. In the roof above the hay-loft, bantams were dozing on beams fat with generations of bantam shit – revolting, hardy little creatures with more in common with dinosaurs than any other known breed of bird. They'd been known to attack rats as they scurried across the floor, hurling themselves onto their backs and pinning them down with their claws while they shredded them with their beaks, spreading the straw with gore, fur and broken bones.

It had amazed Adam as much as anyone that winter when, without so much as a squawk, half a dozen of the bantams had expired from the cold and fallen to the ground with a thump. Even in winters when old women had frozen to death in their cottages, the bantams had always seemed indomitable, buried in their white or red-brown feathers, staring around them with needle-sharp eyes. Adam had almost been pleased to find that they, too, had a breaking point. It was the nakedness of hill farming that appealed to him – the ravages of the cold, the relentless rhythms and cycles that most people went out of their way to avoid.

Adam pulled on his fake Barbour, his sou'wester and his plastic trousers, picked up the bucket and went to the big shed door, bracing himself for the blast of the wind and feeling his muscles swell as he dragged it closed behind him. Outside, it was dark and wild, raindrops chasing like swarming insects in front of the single light bulb on the shed wall. The light glimmered from the water that burst from the guttering, thundered against the drum of the roof, refilled the bucket as he held it beneath the drainpipe, not even bothering to go to the water-butt which was overflowing three and a half feet away.

Pausing to look around him, Adam thought for a moment that he heard the howling of a dog. He frowned and looked towards the kennel at the top of the yard – listening through the sounds of the wind around the roofs and the chimneys – but even though he could hear nothing further, he put the bucket down and set off towards the faintly glowing windows of the house. When a single dead sheep meant wasting hours of back-breaking labour, you couldn't just dismiss the possibility of a stray.

He left the yard and followed the thin path around the back of the house, the wind in the ivy obscuring what sounded again like howling, although still he couldn't be certain. He tramped on through the mud and the rain, peering into the darkness, wondering vaguely how many slates would come off the roof that night, whether they had sufficient spare for him to be able to replace them all in the morning.

Pressed between the ground and the back door, there was some kind of shape: something twitching, dark and dog-sized. "Oh, fucking hell!" said Adam, flinching.

Even in the light from the kitchen window, he couldn't quite believe that it was a human being crumpled on the doorstep, covered in mud, whimpering and clawing at the wood with ripped, bloody fingernails.

"Andrew?" he said. "Andrew... Are you alright?"

He knelt down quickly on the ground and, gently as he could, put a hand on Andrew's shoulder, rolling him onto his back. A short, strangled noise came from the boy's mouth, and he curled himself up into a ball, shaking and whining, but Adam could still see his face – his eyes squeezed closed against the light and the streaming rain, blood in the filth on his cheeks and his forehead.

"You're okay now," said Adam, speaking more softly. "You're safe now, Andrew. Don't worry. It's okay. It's okay..."

He slid his arms beneath the boy's legs and shoulders, and picked him up slowly, resting his head against his chest. Andrew's trousers were torn, worn through at the knees where the calloused flesh was sticky with blood, his black hair matted, twigs and thorns in the tangle of his clothes.

Shaking off his hat and his wellies, Adam opened the door to the boot-passage and carried Andrew through into the warmth of the kitchen, heading for the sink. He had done no more than turn on the hot tap – filling the blue plastic bowl – when there were footsteps on the stairs behind him and Tara came down through the living-room, a pen and her diary in one hand, dressed in her long white nightgown.

"Adam?" she asked. "What is it? What's going on?"

"He..." Adam's voice shook perceptibly. "He was lying on the doormat, and I... I thought he was a dog, Tara! I really thought he was a dog!"

"Oh, Christ!" said Tara. She bent over him, then winced and hurried back upstairs, returning a few moments later with a sponge and a large white towel from the airing cupboard. By this stage, Adam had filled the sink with warm water and had extracted Andrew from his jacket and the too-big boots flapping around his feet. His legs were scratched, horny where the boots had rubbed him, as well as on his hands and knees. The stench beneath his clothes was the stench of dogs. There was filth ingrained into his skin, and when Tara finally managed to remove his cast-off shirt, which itself fell loose to his calves, his chest was thin and his stomach distended.

Andrew was quiet now, his eyes unfocused, still trembling faintly – either from shock, or terror, or confusion. You could see the twitches passing over his body when he came back to himself, but these never transformed into an attempt to escape, and they vanished altogether whenever Tara was holding him, dipping the sponge into the steaming water and washing him as carefully as she could, the grease and grime soon floating around the bowl in clouds.

"I think these are just scratches," said Adam, quietly. "I mean, I think they're from bushes and fences on the way over here. I don't think they happened at home."

"Maybe not," Tara allowed. "But we've got to find out what went on over there. I'm not letting him go back until we know."

Adam lifted Andrew from the edge of the sink and she wrapped him in the big white towel, holding him to her chest and rocking him gently – so subsumed in the folds that he looked like a baby. "No," Adam agreed. "We can't send him back tonight."

"This time," she said. "Adam, we have got to call the social services. I mean, he's a child, for Christ's sake! I don't care if everyone else in the village thinks we're meddling, we've got to do something!"

"Yeah," Adam rubbed his eyes with the balls of his thumbs. "Okay... Look, we'll keep him here tonight, yeah? I'll go back out and check the ewes. Then, if you can keep an eye on them for a bit, I'll drive round to Werndunvan and have a word with Philip, let him know where he's got to. Not that he's probably even noticed. Tomorrow we'll sit down and we'll work out what to do. Okay?"

✳ ✳ ✳

Two hours later, Tara arrived in the shed, still in her nightdress, but with a heavy green coat over the top of it and black wellington boots poking from the bottom. Adam was again washing his hands, in a separate part of the shed, three more lambs shivering in the straw beside him, their wide-eyed faces mirrored by their mother's. On a nearby post, the radio was playing another tribute to John Lennon, its songs and interviews scattered by the wind and the shouts of the ewes.

"He's asleep at last," she said, leaning at the edge of the pen. "So, how was Philip?"

"Well..." Adam washed the last of the afterbirth from his arm, rolling down his sleeve. "To be honest, he really looked quite shaken. I mean, you know what Philip's like. He kept on and on about this bloody shed he's going to build, how he'll be lambing in the dry next year. But he was soaking wet when I got there, and there was mud halfway up his trousers... I'm fairly sure he'd been out looking for him."

"Did you find out what happened?"

"Yeah," Adam sighed. "Well, I think so. He said he'd drowned some puppies this afternoon and that Andrew took it badly. Which, I suppose, adds up... From what I could gather, sometime this evening Dora went out to fetch him in for his tea, and when she couldn't find him in the barn she freaked out completely and had to take her tablets... He must have run over here, in the dark."

"God, what a mess!" said Tara.

"That's about the size of it."

Adam climbed the hurdle, shook a few drops of water from his hands and put his arms around her shoulders. Her face was warm and smooth against his neck, her chest moving at the same, weary pace as his own. Despite the stink of wool and blood that hung about him, he could still smell her hair, sweet and clean, and it made him think about bed, the softness of the pillow, the weight of the duvet. Slowly, he let his hand slide down her back, to the curve at the base of her spine, and as their thighs touched beneath the hem of her coat, his mind filled with thoughts of her legs and her breasts.

Tara shifted her weight, allowing a small space to open between them, then she took half a step backwards. On the post beside them the radio surged and crackled.

"He hasn't got a clue, has he?" she said, eventually.

"None that I've noticed," said Adam. He let his arms drop back to his sides. "I don't think he's hurting him or anything, though... Not in that way... Not intentionally, at least."

Around them, bit by bit, the wind was beginning to die down, its noise sinking from a howl to a moan. Across the shed, a cat jumped from the haystack onto the white-smeared nose of the truck. In a nearby pen, a ewe was turning about herself, bleating with discomfort, treading down the clean straw.

"Are you alright, Adam?" asked Tara, looking at him.

"I'm just tired." Adam managed a smile. "I haven't slept for three days, that's all..."

"How's it looking for tonight?"

"There's one about due, but there should be some peace once she's done."

"Wake me up then." Tara put her hand lightly on his elbow. "Okay? I'll do the rest of the shift. Andrew's clothes will be dry before all that long. I'll bring them down here and do a bit of darning."

\* \* \*

Once Tara had gone, Adam sat on a bale beside a fat ewe in a sheep-shaped nest, her waters dribbling down her pink, swollen udders. From time to time, she would struggle to her feet and circle her pen, letting out cries of alarm, but the contractions were coming faster now and she soon sank back into the straw.

Adam watched her in silence, chewing the stem of his unlit pipe as the ewe rolled onto her side – her eyes turning white as she tried to see behind her, the first black speck of a tiny pair of hooves beginning to appear through the mucus. Even at the end of lambing, when he was so exhausted he could hardly stand upright, Adam was always astonished by the process of birth. He knew these animals almost as well as he knew his own family – their habits, their histories, their faces and fleeces – and the delight he felt when one of them lambed had little to do with economics.

"Good girl," he murmured, tasting the bitter tar in his pipe, keeping himself awake. "Good girl. That's the way..."

The hooves emerged slowly, pressed together, slimy and shiny, and Adam had been watching them for some minutes before he realised that there was anything wrong. Above him, the wind continued to mutter in the roof, curling beneath the sheets of corrugated iron and falling away into the darkness. Holding a hurdle, he pulled himself to his feet and a feeling came over him like he had fallen asleep and something terrible was happening to the farm in his absence. He tried to slow his breathing, afraid that he was about to pass out, but then his thoughts cleared and he climbed into the pen, removing his coat and his jumper, rolling up the sleeves of his shirt.

It was an unusual operation, but one that Adam had performed several times before. The hooves were facing upwards, so the lamb was almost certainly breech – back-to-front, with its hind legs coming out first – and, with the risk it might drown in the amniotic fluid, it was for once critical to hurry. Mumbling soothingly, he washed his hands in the bowl at the edge of the pen and knelt down behind the ewe, watching the fleshy eruption of her vulva, the hooves beginning to evolve into a pair of little white legs.

With the next contraction, Adam took hold of the legs, braced himself and pulled. He drew the lamb straight out towards him, as gently as he could, feeling for any complications. But it came far faster than he had expected and, suddenly, with a cry from the ewe, he found himself holding a steaming pair of legs: perfectly formed, covered in wool, attached to an umbilical cord and completely independent of any other body parts.

For a moment, Adam thought that he had somehow pulled the lamb in half. Slowly he sank backwards, staring at this aberration in his hands, the ewe kicking herself to her feet, and as he dropped the legs into the straw a sense of failure poured over him, a desperate loneliness, a pressure applying itself to the sides of his head. Every disappointment, every setback that he had ever had as a farmer or a father, came flooding through his mind, and by the time that the ewe had turned and was licking the legs with vigorous strokes of her tongue, Adam was hunched on the floor of the pen, his shoulders shivering, his slime-covered hands pressed to his wet face.

# CHAPTER FIVE

# THE
# CLAUDE GLASS

Andrew woke at the same time as always, except that, rather than Meg and the puppies, he was presented with a series of coloured shapes hovering above his head, stirring in the faint breeze from an open door, turning in circles about themselves. They were red, yellow, brown, green, purple, every colour that he could think of, and, as he stared at them, he saw that one had the same shape as a sheep – in fact, it had the colours of a sheep, as well. It was a thin little sheep that was performing its twirls above him, and it was surrounded by other animals, none of which he recognised, with unfamiliar teeth, hair, claws and feathers.

Andrew was about to reach up for the sheep, to see if he could touch it, when he felt a pain in his arm and realised that it was covered in some kind of thick white material, and that beneath it his skin was burning, as were his knees and other patches all over his body. In a moment, he made the connection between the material and the pain, and he went to tear it off, but his fingernails too were covered, so he grabbed it with his teeth, uncovering swellings the whole way to his elbow, before – with a start – he noticed the room he was in, and looked around.

The room was light, lit by a big white ball which hung from the ceiling, and a trace of the sunrise crept around the curtains. He was lying in a bed, but the bed was small – not like the huge, stinking object where he sometimes slept between his parents – and there were nothing but blankets to either side of him: warm but lifeless, with scarcely a smell of their own.

Andrew sat up, shuffled forwards along the bed and discovered that, as well as the thick white material, he was wearing a thin striped suit which fitted him precisely. Confused, he moved closer to the window and, not wanting to touch the curtains, he peered through the crack beside the wall, seeing the lovely curves of Offa's Bank through glass so clear that it might not have been there at all. He saw pools of light, flooding across the valley, shapeless and changing against the lines of the fields. He saw sheep still crammed beneath the trees, the hazy green of the chestnuts, the fat, spiky catkins in the pussy willows. Then the clouds shifted away from him, and the sun was poised above the nose of the hill, round and perfect, forcing him back into the shadows of the room.

Climbing out of bed, Andrew found that the floor was soft, light and colourful as everything seemed to be, here on the other side of the hill. The smells were strange and subtle, so that sometimes he could barely smell them at all. There was a sheepskin on a chair beside the door, a whiff of old tobacco smoke, a heap of clean clothes on the floor, wood, stone and plaster somewhere in the background, dry and redolent.

He crossed the carpet to the bare floorboards and went through the door, his feet white-cushioned, moving softly. Outside, other doors lined a narrow passage where a staircase sank into the floor, and there was the faint, familiar smell of urine. As in the abandoned rooms in Werndunvan, there was a second staircase that went upwards – light was spilling around it – but Andrew thought only about going down, about returning to the ground, and he took the handrail, rounded the banisters and descended a stair at a time.

At the bottom, there were still no sounds, except for the faraway calls of the sheep. Andrew stopped and looked around him, inspecting the three doors that it was possible to take, the carpet of fabulous, swirling patterns that lay in the middle of the floor, the tall, heavy piece of furniture that stood against one of the walls, a long flat lip at its front and a threadbare stool tucked beneath it, just like the one that he had seen at Werndunvan.

Among the shadows, Andrew saw the face of a man looking down at him: neat, grey and severe-looking. Around the man was a square of shiny wood, and there were papers and pieces of machinery on the table in front of him. Andrew looked at the man's face, his long thin nose, his shining green eyes, and in them he saw the yellow-haired woman who had taken his hand when the tractors got stuck, who had washed him and held him, and a feeling of warmth came over him, filling him so entirely that, for a moment, he forgot about everything else.

It was only the frightened, unexpected smell of a lamb that jerked Andrew back into the hall, and his mind turned instantly to lambing time, to minding the tiddlers – one of the few tasks he had ever been given. He sniffed the air eagerly, trying to work out where the smell was coming from, then he looked around at the sun-filled door behind him and headed towards it.

\* \* \*

Robin woke Martin the moment that he woke himself, and, shivering slightly and kicking his damp sheet and pyjama bottoms towards the foot of the bed, he resumed the story that they'd been inventing before they went to sleep. As usual, the story concerned the Sheenah – their villainous enemy – and their voyages through kingdoms full of dragons, gold and castles. But, for once, Robin couldn't quite lose himself in it. He thought it odd that Tara hadn't come in to wake them, lambing time or not, and he couldn't help wondering if anything was wrong.

The boys' bedroom was small and its curtains showed many horsemen with spears pursuing many tigers through the oriental jungle. It had a crowded bookshelf, several teddy bears and a chest of drawers, which Robin had written his name all over with a red crayon, leaving only the underwear drawer, where he had written Martin's name instead. He slept in the bed next to the door, because Martin was afraid that a monster might come through it in the night and was pathetically grateful to be able to sleep against the wall. Besides, Robin reasoned, any monster worth the name would obviously not bother with the door, but would come bursting through the wall, if only to prove the point.

"Morning, boys!" said Tara, appearing in the doorway, opening the curtains on a dazzling morning of ripped-apart clouds. "Time to get up!"

Robin handed her the bedclothes, which she tossed into the basket on the landing.

"We've got a guest for breakfast," said Tara.

"Who?" asked Robin.

"Andrew," said Tara.

"The werewolf!" said Martin, and a range of little ridges appeared across his forehead, his face turning red, as if he was about to cry.

"What?" Tara looked confused. "What do you mean?"

"Andrew's a werewolf!" exclaimed Martin. "Klaus said! He said he's going to turn into a wolf and come and eat our brains!"

"Oh, Martin..." Tara sighed. She knelt down and looked at him, his tears making snail-trails on his cheeks. "Listen to me," she said, gently. "I don't care what Klaus said, okay? That's not true, and it's not a kind thing to say about anyone. Andrew is a normal boy. He's a normal boy who's having a lot of trouble right now, and it isn't fair to be nasty about him... You wouldn't want people to be nasty about you, would you?"

\* \* \*

Robin and Martin descended the stairs in a different way to their mother. Halfway down, there was a stair which squeaked like an old gate, and ever since Mr Gwynne had taught him about Roundheads and Cavaliers at school Robin had insisted they use the banisters and the skirting board to climb around it. In all great houses, there was always a priest's hole, a secret tunnel to the nearest church, and a special stair which would make the whole staircase collapse if you so much as touched it. There was no point in taking any chances.

The two of them followed Tara to the door into the kitchen where, in front of the Aga, across the red tile floor, Andrew was sitting in a large cardboard box, dressed in Robin's spare blue and green pyjamas, cradling a lamb that had been born sometime that morning, feeding it from a wine-bottle with a pink rubber teat on the end.

Neither of them looked up.

"Tara?" Robin whispered. "Andrew's wearing my pyjamas!"

"That's okay, isn't it, Robin?" said Tara, carrying a heap of plates to the table and laying them out, collecting a couple of old ones and depositing them in the sink. "The boys were going to have a bit of breakfast now, Andrew. What do you think? Would you like some breakfast?"

Slowly, Andrew looked up at her, his face round and pink, with surprisingly pale blue eyes. He watched her for a moment or two, then returned his attention to the lamb – so obviously content that Robin wondered if he'd imagined all of the events at the bog the other day. He imagined so many things that sometimes he really wasn't sure. Andrew was not as hairy as he'd remembered, nor did he have particularly sharp teeth. He looked, in fact, very much like a normal boy.

"Come on, Robbo," Tara continued. "Come and sit down. And you, Mart."

Robin hesitated, burning to go and play with the lamb, inspecting Andrew's lowered head, his mop of black hair, while Martin darted past him, climbed up onto the bench and crawled quickly to the other end. Andrew's hands, arms and feet were covered in an impressive number of plasters and bandages. He was holding the lamb on his lap just as Adam had taught Robin the previous year and, if you listened carefully, he was making quiet sheep noises, which Robin had never tried himself.

"Robbo..." Tara repeated, pointedly. "I've put some wheat flakes out on the table, and... Here, I'll do you some toast as well."

Cutting a few slices from one of her wholemeal loaves, she laid them on the Aga to toast, and when Andrew still didn't move she bent down and whispered to him, taking the lamb from his arms and sitting it beside him on the layers of old newspaper, where it bleated a couple of times and promptly fell asleep. She took his hand and led him to the table, lifting him up onto a cushion-heaped chair and placing a piece of toast and honey in front of him.

Andrew seemed to gawp at the cutlery, at the wheat flakes, the sugar, milk and butter spread across the wide oak table, sniffing at the strands of smoke still rising from his plate. But then he glanced at Tara, who smiled, and he took the toast in both hands and began to eat it as quickly as possible, cramming his mouth and mumbling with pleasure.

Sitting on the bench, Robin watched him with amazement. He longed to stuff his food down like that, without Tara telling him off, and once Andrew had finished – more alert-looking suddenly, checking around him to see if there was any more on its way – he decided that perhaps he ought to talk to him, so as not to be nasty, as Tara had said.

"Nice tractor your dad's got, Andrew," he offered.

Andrew looked up, questioningly, and sniffed again at the bread now cooking on the Aga.

"The Mercedes," said Robin.

Andrew's face cleared. He nodded, smiled and got to work on another piece of toast as Tara delivered it to his plate – glancing at Robin as she handed him his own piece, smiling herself with her shining green eyes.

\* \* \*

Andrew had various dens about Werndunvan – places where his father couldn't fit, places forgotten behind haystacks or rotting pieces of machinery where the cats or chickens went to nest and any normal person could pass you daily and never once notice you were there. The only constraint was the seasons, which left the dingle down behind the house miserable and sodden in the wintertime, the scramble of strange trees and shrubs in the garden leafless and exposed. Outside of the summer, the best places were always in the barns, or in the other parts of the house – behind the door in the sitting-room where Philip hung his coats, never seeming to notice that the house continued, and continued.

Andrew flicked up the catch on the end door, poking it with the stick that he kept against the door jamb, rubbing Meg's neck for a moment before he left her on the doorstep, curled in the pale sunlight with her teats still swollen and the sounds of a JCB working on the new barn a little way along the hill.

With the door closed, the smells changed abruptly: there was so much dust and dirt everywhere that it was almost like snow, although if you went up the decaying stairs in front of you there were rooms where broken windows left the floors slick with rain, where white mould flowered on the walls and furniture and the wind blew just as furiously as it did outside. But Andrew went forwards, as he always went forwards, into a short passage with a couple of small, musty rooms to his left, past the tall man in tight trousers who lived on the wall, bars of curling black hair on his red cheeks and Werndunvan alone on its hillside behind him, lacking its pines and its barns.

At the end of the passage – behind a large, solid door – was the biggest room that Andrew had found. It looked out at the yard through dirty windows, patched so the dust stayed thick and undisturbed on the floor, coating the boxes and the sheets on the big, shiny chairs. From the ceiling, a fabulous construction – scores of dusty glass-drops – swung faintly, turning the sunlight into colours on the facing wall.

Recently, Andrew had opened the door into this room for the first time, and he had noticed from his foot-prints that the floor was composed of tiny pieces of wood. He had been thinking about Robin, as he did much of the time these days, about Tara and breakfast at Penllan, and, while he thought, he had swept away the dust with his hands – discovering how perfectly each piece of the floor fitted with the last, their little arrangement repeating itself in twists and circles all around him.

No matter how far he progressed across the room, Andrew found the same, beautiful pattern, and as he was following it, tracing the cracks with his fingernails, he came across an object beneath the dust: rectangular, bound in a kind of black skin, the size of his two hands put together. Andrew picked the object up. He polished it on the sleeve of his jacket, turning it with interest and inspecting the little gold latch on its side, the frayed corners where the skin had come away to reveal the wood beneath it.

Fiddling with the latch, the object fell open, and, holding it up, Andrew was presented with a small, dark face, staring at him from the shadows across the room. He moved his head to one side, looking around the object, waiting for a movement to reveal where the person had gone. Yet, when he looked back at it, there was the face again, gawping at him with its wild dark hair, its mouth hanging open as if it was taunting him.

Andrew became confused. He dropped the object and peered with swelling panic at the door where the person must have disappeared. He had heard nothing, no voice or footsteps, either of the person coming or of them going away again. But then, there were noises everywhere, once he started to listen: the hiss of his breathing, the thin bleats of lambs in the shed, the wind sucking round the walls and corners of the yard, the grinding of machinery in the bottom field. Perhaps, after all, he had simply been too immersed to notice.

After a minute or two, Andrew became more confident that whoever it was had gone, or that perhaps he had imagined it all, and his thoughts slipped back towards the object on the floor in front of him. He picked it back up and inspected it in more detail, stroking each part with his fingers and murmuring to himself. Around the corners, the outside skin stopped almost immediately. The object had become a pair of thinner rectangles with a pair of gold hinges between them. One of these rectangles was lined in a soft, smooth material which his fingers found delicious. The other was a sheet made of some kind of glass, although unlike any glass that Andrew had ever seen. It was shiny, rounded slightly towards him, and it was black.

Around it was a thin golden border, wrinkled and ornate, like the one around the man on the wall by the staircase.

\* \* \*

"You two wait here a moment," said Tara distractedly, opening the car door for Robin, waiting as he sat down next to Martin. "I've just got to have a word with Mr Gwynne, okay?"

Robin watched as she leant against the jagged-topped wall next to the large grey playground, where Mr Gwynne was waiting for her, playing with his glasses. Beyond them, squeezed beneath the end of Offa's Bank, the school was solid and fringed in white, with a red-brick extension poking from its side and a bell-tower sitting on the roof. Tara had one leg tucked behind the other, her hair hanging straight down the sides of her face so it was hard to see her expression, but when she turned round to check on them her eyes seemed worried and a frown line was running down her forehead.

"Look, Robin!" said Martin, who was playing with a model crossbow that Adam had made for him. "Look! Look how far I can fire a matchstick!"

A horrible cold feeling was trickling through Robin's stomach at the thought that he was being talked about, and the longer he watched, the worse it became. Looking back inside the car, he noticed a neatly folded tartan blanket on the front seat, where he and Martin weren't allowed to sit, and suddenly he had an idea.

"I know, Mart," he said. "Let's make a den!"

He grabbed the blanket and tossed the edge over the back of the grey-blue seat, the two of them pulling the rest over their heads, tucking in the corners so the only light was the reds and the browns of its pattern. It made Robin feel better almost immediately – apart from the outside world, like when they climbed inside the duvet cover.

"Where shall we go?" he asked.

"Wales," said Martin, definitely.

"Yes, but what castle?"

"I want to see the castle on the rock!" said Martin. "Harley Castle. And I want to see some dungeons!"

"Harlech," Robin corrected him.

Ever since he had borrowed Mr Gwynne's picture book on castles, Robin had decided that he was a world-famous expert on the subject, and that Martin could ask him anything he liked about it and he would always know the answer. Most of all, he liked to talk about the castles of Wales – hung with mist and steeped in legend – but he had recently found out about Crac des Chevaliers in the Holy Land, too, and already he had drawn himself a big, colourful map, and he was working out the best way to walk there.

"Harlech Castle is in North Wales," Robin began. "It's on a great big cliff near the seaside, and no one can attack us because we've got a drawbridge and we can pour boiling oil on them!"

"Has it got dungeons?" asked Martin.

"Yes," Robin nodded, "but we're the only ones

who know where they are. No one else has ever found them!"

"Has it got treasure?" asked Martin. "Robin? Has it? Has it got treasure?"

In all of their stories, there had to be treasure. The two boys longed for it and looked for it everywhere – beneath the barns and at the old quarries up on Cold Winter, because clearly someone had been digging for something there and, no matter what Adam said, no one was going to go and dig up ordinary stone. Cold Winter was the perfect place to build a castle – even Mr Gwynne said that – so perhaps the whole hill was a labyrinth of vaulted passages, abandoned for centuries like the cave beneath Snowdon where Arthur and his knights were awaiting their time to return.

There was a clunk from the car door and Tara sat down in the driver's seat, wiggling the gearstick before she started the engine.

"I'm not sure," she was saying through the window. "They said they'd try and get round there next week sometime."

"Keep me posted, anyway," said Mr Gwynne.

"Try and get round where, Tara?" said Martin.

Peeping from the side of the blanket, Robin discovered that Tara was smiling. So perhaps they hadn't been talking about him, after all.

"You know what, boys?" said Tara, pulling away towards the first corner where you could see Penllan isolated on the hillside. "A long, long time ago, some really quite famous people used to stay at Andrew's house. The

sister of a famous poet and all sorts... He's an interesting man, your teacher." She paused. "You're a lucky boy,
Robin. Do you know that?"

Robin nodded at the mirror on the windscreen and
fastened his seatbelt before she had to tell him, so she
would like him even more. Then he turned his eyes
to the telegraph wire rising and falling beside the car,
which he often imagined travelling along with a pulley.
Or maybe two, so he could swap them when he got to
the poles.

"You've had a good day, then?" asked Tara.

"We learnt all about sieges," said Robin. "We learnt
how you can dig a hole under the corner of a castle, then
you can put in wooden stakes to hold it up, and then you
can build a great big fire in the hole so the stakes all burn
and the whole corner of the castle falls down!"

As he stopped talking, Robin had a feeling that Tara
was about to broach something and he felt scared again
and fell silent, watching her eyes in the reflection, which
in turn were watching the road. They followed the sweep
between a buttress of the hill and a ramshackle piece of
woodland belonging to Bill Llanoley, the indicator ticking
next to the steering wheel as they turned left onto the
track, bumping over the lumps and the potholes.

In the field to their left, lambs were streaking round
the fences and hedgerows, climbing mounds and becoming monarchs, burying themselves beneath their mothers
the instant anyone came too close.

"Robbo," said Tara, in the voice that Robin had
been hoping desperately she wouldn't use. "Do you think

you can tell me about this Sheenah thing? What is it all about?" She paused, then noticed his face. "I'm not cross with you..."

"The Sheenah's the enemy," said Robin, trying not to start crying.

"Well, what do they look like?" asked Tara. "Where do they come from?"

Robin actually liked talking about the Sheenah a great deal, and he felt a little better. He glanced at her in the mirror, her eyes looking steadily at the track, the dingle around them an impenetrable mess of trees and dead ferns, nettles and brambles.

"The Sheenah come from England," he said. "The other side of Offa's Dyke, where they cut the ears off Welshmen!"

"They drive a Ford Granada," added Martin, who didn't like to be left out of things.

"And they wear caps with peaks," said Robin, "and they've got guns, but they can't do anything because we're going to build a trebuchet and we'll squash them with a rock!"

"Yeah!" said Martin.

"Robbo," said Tara. "I'm not telling you off, okay? I like you making up stories and everything, but there are one or two children in your class you've been telling about the Sheenah, and they've got themselves into a bit of a state about it. I know that Mr Gwynne has had to talk to you today. Debbie's mother isn't very happy, because Debbie has started having nightmares that these Sheenah people are coming to attack her..."

Robin started crying, quietly, the tears tickling as they trickled down his face. He could have told Tara that the Sheenah were indeed about to come and attack Debbie, but his throat was all tight and he couldn't make the words come out. They rolled up the last bit of the track, past the vegetable garden, past the laburnum tree which flowered yellow in the summer and Tara had told them never to touch, and came to a halt beneath the woodshed.

"Look," Tara turned round to face him. The hand-brake ratcheted. "You're a big boy now, Robbo, and Mr Gwynne is very pleased with you. He thinks you're doing very well indeed. But if you're going to tell stories, you can't just tell them like they're true. Okay? Because that's a bit like lying. It upsets people, and you don't want to go round upsetting people, do you now, eh?"

\* \* \*

One good thing about wearing such a large jacket was that Andrew could put the object in his pocket and fit his hand in there as well, so he could play with it as he was wandering around the place. He loved the feeling of the two sides: the soft, furry cushioning which you could press down with your finger and feel as it rose up again, the cool, clean smoothness of the glass. At first, he had stroked the glass with his fingertips, following its curve from frame to frame, but his fingers were often sticky and more than anything he loved the feeling when the glass was clean. So now he always touched it with his fingernails, sliding them across it ceaselessly, the surface as slippery as ice.

Andrew got such a shock when Philip appeared in the barn and took his hand that he very nearly wet himself. As with the person whose face he had seen in the big, abandoned room, he had somehow failed to hear him coming – dizzy with pleasure, immersed in the feel of the glass until the dogs, the hay, the smells and the sounds of the world had fallen clear away from him. The fact that his father was actually holding his hand only struck Andrew as he was being marched down the yard beside him, his fingers buried in the huge hard grip.

"Hell, but she's a machine!" Philip was saying as he dragged him round the corner at the bottom of the barn, through the gate towards the site of the new shed. "You ain't never seen nothing like her, boy. I swear to fucking God you ain't!"

He stopped abruptly at the top of the new cutting, where the ground was scarred with the tooth-marks of the diggers. A JCB was working away, tidying off the edges of the new ledge, loading earth into an enormous lorry. But it was past them that Philip was looking, to the new stretch of track that looped down the hill from the yard, where an entirely new scale of machinery shook the ground around it.

"A bulldozer, Andrew!" said Philip, his voice transported with excitement. "A bulldozer! Will you just look at her, boy!"

Every tremor in Philip's voice, every twitch in his hand, Andrew felt completely. He watched the bulldozer in a rapture, seeing it slice through the old field – the grass, the earth, the stones underneath it – shoving them all aside as if they were dust.

"We've got to have a ride on her!" Philip went on. "Think about it, boy! We could change the whole farm around, we could! Make everything just exactly how we want it!"

While the two of them were gazing from the muddy cliff top – still holding hands, dressed as ever in the same flat caps, the same threadbare jackets, the same muddy boots that Andrew might one day swell to occupy – a car appeared on the track to the left, weaving around the holes, windscreen wipers whirring against the spitting rain and the fat black clouds. Neither of them noticed it until it stopped at the last gate, and the driver got out and began to walk towards them.

He was a tall man with a beard and long hair tied up like a woman's on the back of his head. As he approached, he was looking at Andrew, not at his father, not at the bulldozer working to his left, and suddenly Andrew was confused again when moments earlier everything had been clean and beautiful.

"Good... morning," said the man, glancing at his wrist. He smiled. "Mr Tolland? And, you're Andrew, right?"

Philip dropped Andrew's hand and advanced a few paces. He had a way of holding his arms out slightly to either side of him when he was getting angry, and, looking at the man, Andrew felt the same, defiant anger growing in himself. For once, rather than shrinking away, he took a couple of paces forward as well, watching the man, his head twisted slightly to one side.

"I'm from the soc—" said the man.

"I don't care where you're from!" barked Philip. "Get the fuck out of my yard!"

"I'm sorry," said the man. "You don't under—"

"Oh, I understand you right enough! Get the fuck out of my yard! Go on, fuck off!"

The man hesitated, glancing behind him at his car.

"Fuck off!" Philip repeated, advancing another step.

"Fuck off!" shouted Andrew.

The man turned without another word and hurried back towards the gate. Andrew shook with excitement. Philip turned and stared down at him with an expression of astonishment, becoming delight – the yellowed teeth exposed in his mouth and the lines bunched up around his eyes.

"What did you just say, boy?" he asked.

Andrew became crushed with fear and embarrassment. Whatever mood had just possessed him had deserted him just as quickly, and all that he could think of was the quiet sweet smells of the hay in the barn, the smoothness of the glass, the warmth of the dogs.

"Go on, Andy," said Philip. "What did you just say?"

"Fuck off," squeaked Andrew, one hand kneading the cushioning in his pocket, his shoulders crumpled, his eyes on the puddles.

As they went down the new track to see the bulldozer, Andrew was riding on Philip's shoulders. He didn't know what had just happened, how he had got there, what any of it meant at all. Far down below on the ground, he could see Meg trailing along behind them, Vaughn and the other dogs joining her as they returned from chasing the man away along the track. The rain had stopped now, and strands of sunlight were moving over the great, dark hills across the valley.

\* \* \*

Over Friday afternoon and Friday night, the roaring became gradually louder, until by Saturday morning – caught by the wind that swirled over the hill – it was all but deafening. Robin was running down the yard as it resumed, tearing through the air and water that funnelled through the space between the barns, hitting him in a wave which almost carried him upwards into the air, as it did in his dreams, when he soared out over the valley, catching the updraught from Offa's Bank like the buzzards, sliding back into Wales, above the hills.

Robin loved running in the wind and the rain so much that he even had a uniform for the purpose. For a time, he had worn a hat – an old flat cap of his father's – but this had kept slipping down over his eyes, or blowing off altogether, so now he had reduced things to a favourite jumper with purple zigzags, a long black mackintosh that had once belonged to Stuart, John the Glyn's son, and a stopped watch which he'd found in a trunk in the attic. It was crucial that everything felt right when you were running in the wind and the rain: any compromise, anything to irritate or distract you, and the point of the whole exercise was lost.

The roaring started just as Robin was returning up the yard, a lightness in his limbs and the air beginning to swell beneath him. He paused among the weeds, beneath the brick face of the workshop, and listened a moment. The noise was like thunder, shaking the ground. It was as if some monstrous tractor had come to life on the hill and was taking its revenge on humanity.

Robin turned and ran up the path behind the house, past a farm cat lying on the wall with half-closed eyes, the daffodils jostling on the bank opposite the woodshed. He ran up the track beneath the small, vivid leaves of the chestnut, jumped the radiator serving as a drainage grille, climbed the gate and was halfway across the following field before it occurred to him that perhaps this really was the noise of some kind of monster, or the terrible Sheenah, and, even if it wasn't, then he ought at least to be careful. He slowed to a walk and peered at the gate in front of him, where he could see the corner of the ruined cottage on the boundary, the cottage's three little damson trees and the beginnings of the old track that ran over the hilltop to Werndunvan: a groove through the field, rutted and grass-covered, lined with ancient, budding hawthorns.

Robin hated change. He had hated it when the old black barn was demolished to make way for the new shed, when the little red combine harvester was sent away on the back of a lorry, when he and Martin had been forced to move bedrooms because Adam had wanted to rebuild one of the walls - even if there had been some kind of wattle and daub behind the plasterboard of the exact same kind used by peasants in the Middle Ages.

After about a hundred yards, the track stopped. An immense yellow machine was working its way towards him, its tracks churning around it, the blade on its front cutting beneath the old hawthorn trees and tearing them from the ground, throwing them away down the slope where their roots and their twigs twitched hopelessly in the wind.

\* \* \*

If the wind was strong on the ground, so Adam had always said, then that was nothing to how strong it would be up in the clouds. Up in the clouds – the fields of grey, white and black where you could make out anything from tractors to dragons – the forces were so powerful that sails would have burst, windmills would have been shattered, and no man could have stood upright even if there had been somewhere for him to put his feet. And this was the place where the buzzards would fly out of choice! You wouldn't see them fluttering around the flowers with the bees and the butterflies. No, they were right up there in the gales, in the regions as cold as the Arctic, circling calmly above the blue-green spaces of the earth!

Robin came flying down the track, beneath the chestnut tree, heading for the woodshed where Adam was turning a sheep's skull in his hands, explaining the plates of the cranium while Martin prodded at the traces of nerves and blood vessels, the cavities of the eyes, asking questions with an expression that suggested he understood every word of what he was hearing.

Martin managed to assume this expression almost every time that he was being taught anything. A few months earlier, he had even convinced their grandfather that he knew how to read – selecting only books that he knew by heart, speaking with absolute conviction – and it had only been when he failed to turn a page at quite the right time that their grandfather had realised he was being duped.

"Adam!" called Robin, almost hysterically, scrambling over the gate. "Adam! Philip's bulldozing the track! He's killing all the hawthorns! He's going to bulldoze the cottage, and the damsons!"

Adam stood upright, replaced the skull in its position on the wall, removed his cap and scraped the other hand through the peak of hair at the top of his forehead.

"It is starting to look that way," he said.

"But—" said Robin. "But, he can't just bulldoze everything like that! It's not right!"

"I agree." Adam put his hat back on his head. "But I'm afraid it is his farm. Look, I'll tell you what. I was just on my way to have a word with him, so why don't the two of you come along? Let's see if we can't do anything to save the cottage. What do you think?"

The three of them returned beneath the chestnut tree, crossed the narrow field beyond it, and Robin and Martin slid with the dogs between the two bottom bars of the gate while Adam swung himself over the top, frowning at the great yellow bulldozer which was working its way steadily down the hill, tearing at the ruts and the roots, its blade close to the lid of the Penllan reservoir, whose spring rose on Werndunvan land.

To the left, the ruined cottage consisted of a pair of gables and a simple back wall, its face open to the fields, a couple of beams and half of the old upper floor drooping forwards, as if revealing themselves to passers-by.

As they started up the untouched stretch of track that led away from the gate, past the three damson trees, Philip stopped the engine and, with a shudder, the mighty machine fell silent. Climbing stiffly from his seat, he called out something to Andrew, who turned and looked down the slope towards them, sitting against one of the unearthed hawthorns, cradling what appeared to be a puppy, rolling and writhing in his lap.

"Philip." Adam nodded, his voice once again in its Radnorshire slur, the dogs swarming between them. "Another fine machine you got there!"

"Ar," said Philip, climbing down, pulling his pipe from his pocket. He glanced back at Andrew. "She's a beauty, alright."

"New puppy and all," said Adam.

"New puppy, ar." Philip tapped the pipe against the tracks beside him. "Di, her name is, after that Lady Di. Come from Bill's litter, she did... Come on, Andy, let Mr Adam and the boys have a look at her now!"

Andrew was bunched between the broken branches of the hawthorn, his head held down so that his eyes and nose were concealed beneath the peak of his cap, and it was only with the greatest reluctance that he got to his feet and allowed Di to bound towards them, following her with hesitant steps and stopping a few yards away.

"The way I figures it," said Philip, as Robin and Martin crowded around the puppy, running their hands through her clean, soft fur, "I've got a dog, the boy should have a dog... If he wants one, look."

"Sounds right enough to me," agreed Adam, his face impassive.

"Andy!" said Philip, speaking with sudden authority. "Tell Mr Adam what you said to the long-hair man!"

Andrew shrank back a couple of paces, lowering his head still further until his mouth disappeared entirely, his hand twitching noticeably in the pocket of his enormous jacket.

"Andy!" said Philip again.

"Fuck off!" squeaked Andrew abruptly. "Fuck off!"

Robin looked at him, astonished. Coming from the mouth of someone very nearly his own age, such a grown-up thing to say seemed about as impressive and remarkable as if he had just lit a pipe, or driven away on a tractor.

"Did you really say that, Andy?" said Adam, looking directly at him.

"Answer Mr Adam," Philip instructed.

Andrew squirmed a bit and then peeped out quickly from beneath the peak of his cap, glancing from them to his puppy, who was busily attacking Martin's wellies.

"Ar," he said, almost silently.

"Well," said Adam. His face was hidden as he rooted in his pockets. He lit his pipe, then he held out the match for Philip to light his own. "So what's the plan with the track, then, Philip?"

"Opening up the field up, I am," said Philip, through the smoke. "Them fucking hawthorns been getting in my way long as I can remember."

Adam nodded, his pipe between his teeth.

"And what about the old cottage there?" he asked. "What you thinking about him?"

Robin picked up Andrew's puppy, rubbing his nose in her coat. His thoughts were full of the dead hawthorns, the clumps of earth clinging to their roots and the bright white cuts where the bulldozer had pulled them from their home beneath the ground. But Adam was here, and he sounded – as usual – so composed that a tidal wave might have crashed over Cold Winter, carrying trees, sheep and neighbours, and he would scarcely have lifted an eyebrow.

"Tell you what, boys," said Adam, pausing in his conversation with Philip. "Why don't you three go off and play for a bit? Just while me and Philip chew these few things over."

"Good idea," said Philip. "Off you go now, Andy. You go off and play with the boys now."

\* \* \*

Andrew kept checking behind him as the three of them set off back down the hill towards the ruined cottage, his movements so reluctant that Robin wanted to keep checking behind himself, as well – afraid that there was something there even more terrible than the huge, sleeping dragon of the bulldozer, the slew of mud and slaughtered hawthorns spread across the hillside. Looking ahead of them, you could almost have thought that the field was completely unchanged. The trees were budding as happily as ever, and the cottage sat square against the hedgerow, surrounded by the same scattered stones and sheep-chewed weeds.

Andrew walked with an oddly lolloping motion, bending down regularly to stroke Di as she bounded around them, his left hand rarely swinging in time with his legs, while his right hand stayed thrust into the pocket of his jacket, working more and more furiously the further away they became from Philip and Adam. He was a similar kind of height to Robin, but because his head was hanging forward he seemed a good bit shorter. Most of the time, you could see nothing beneath the peak of his cap, except for his mouth, which remained open constantly – catching flies, as their grandfather would have put it – his tongue pressed against his bottom lip like he was panting.

"Have you ever been spinning, Andrew?" asked Robin finally, when the boundary gate was ominously close. "It's really good fun!"

"Yeah, let's go spinning!" said Martin.

Robin climbed the bank to their left and stood between a pair of hawthorns, their twigs shivering and waving in the air above him. He looked down the slope, towards the thicker greens and patches of grey sky reflected in the bog, the woods and the string of the three ponds – which soon became a stream, following the dingle the length of the valley until it merged with the brook in the village, where the older boys liked to go fishing after school.

"Spinning's easy," Robin explained. He turned around a couple of times. "All you have to do is spin round and round and go down the hill. You've got to try and stay upright for as long as you can, and you've got to keep your hands out of your pockets or else you might hurt yourself when you fall over. Okay?"

He lined the three of them between the two hawthorns, and when he glanced at Andrew he had removed his hand from his jacket pocket and was watching him warily, his pale eyes hovering beneath the brim of his flat cap.

"Are you ready, then?" he said. "We'll go when I say three. Okay? One... two... three!"

Spinning was compulsive once you started to do it – a bit like running in the wind and the rain, except that it made the world become detached altogether. There was no way of soaring when the ground was pitching and wheeling around you, like it was vanishing down some enormous plughole, when your feet were stumbling uncontrollably through thistles and molehills, when your mind was full of a sickening elation and the earth was switching roles with the sky.

Lying in a quivering heap on the hillside, the ground still heaving and keeling beneath him, his legs and his arms strewn in every direction, Robin could hear an extraordinary noise coming from somewhere nearby and he tried to lift his head to see what on earth it could be. The noise was chattering and hysterical, like some kind of bird, and when Robin did finally manage to look up he realised that Andrew was lying face-down a little way on down the hill, giggling into the grass, and he could feel the specks of the drizzle landing gently on his left cheek although everything else in his body seemed to be revolving at a terrible rate.

Andrew had lost his cap a good way back up towards the track, past even Martin, who had fallen over after only a few seconds and was now wrestling with Di, blowing into her ear so that she jumped and growled around him. There were other things strewn down the slope where Andrew had been spinning – a few scraps of paper which the wind was carrying away towards the hedge, a length of orange baler twine, some straw, stones, nails and, not a foot or two from Robin's head, a funny little black leather case with a hook-and-eye clasp on its front.

Robin pushed himself upright, checked to see if Andrew was watching him, then picked up the case and wiped it on the sleeve of his mackintosh, inspecting it carefully. The case looked old – its leather was peeling at the corners, and the wood peering through from underneath was riddled with tiny holes. Robin turned it over in his hands several times before he opened the catch, and revealed a rectangle of black velvet on one side and on the other a small black mirror surrounded by a gold-painted frame. It was curved towards him, Robin realised, and when he held it close to his face his reflection was like looking in the back of a spoon, his nose grown huge, while his ears, his hair and his chin were tiny and comical around the edges.

But then there was the frame and, turning the mirror away from him slightly, Robin found Offa's Bank lying neatly within it – its sweeping shape pressed low by a grey-black sky, the detail of its trees and its hedges lost among the dark, mysterious colours. It was a portable picture that Andrew was carrying around with him! A funny little mirror, which could turn their valley into something foreign and far away!

# CHAPTER SIX

# BUT THEN
# FACE TO FACE

Andrew sat with Di in the hayloft, back in the corner at the top of the bale elevator, as far as he could get from the winds that crowded through the door and made long sad notes in the slits in the thick stone walls. It was cold again, one of those days that had never quite been convinced of itself and was now limping off as fast as possible. The light outside was drab and watery. The light bulb next to the kitchen window was weak in its little glass shell, the puddle of green mould at its bottom one of the few definite colours. Once in a while, one of the people at the front door pressed themselves to the window, side-lit, but even their colourful clothing scarcely stood out amongst the browns and greys.

In his mind, Andrew kept spinning. He spun from the bare ground where there had once been a track to Penllan, he spun down the smoothed-out fields on the side of Cold Winter, he spun down the bank beneath the yard. For unknown periods of time, he stayed in the big, clean house across the hill, sleeping in the bed with the colourful spinning shapes above his head, eating in the warm red kitchen, where Tara would smile at him and tell him what to do in every moment – the mere idea of which made him feel light, like he felt when the lambs were born, when the trees began to bud, when the smells in the air ceased to be merely the smells of damp, cold and decay and became the smells of growth and sunshine as well.

In the yard, the man and the woman had given up knocking on the front door and had retreated a few paces, whispering to one another between the brightening light bulb and the elongated, shadowy figures that lay across the puddles and the half-chewed mud. Andrew lifted Di gently from his lap and laid her on the bales, stroking her for a moment, trying not to wake her. He crawled a few feet closer to the nearest slit, and looked down at the man with the hair like a woman's, the woman whose own hair grew outwards in a giant mass, glowing at the edges when she walked in front of the light bulb.

Andrew knew already that it was going to thunder. He had known for some time – in the same way that he knew when he was hungry, or when he needed to go to sleep. The thunder grew in him, as it grew in the air and the wind around them. It scared him in ways that he couldn't hold in his mind. It was the animal at the door with the yellow eyes, the face that had gawped at him in the room with the pattern for a floor, these people in the yard, calling his name periodically, hunting him down to his den.

Once, when they were still in one piece, Philip had closed the doors to the barn every night. The doors were oak, an inch and a half thick, tall as a combine harvester, hanging from enormous iron hinges. During thunderstorms, in the darkness, the lightning had surrounded them as if the house itself had exploded and the barn was about to fall in on the clustered, shivering animals inside. The dogs hated thunderstorms, they hated them so much that they would howl at the leaking roof, at the damp stone walls, and Meg would throw herself at the doors in a frenzy, tearing at them with her claws, until one night she had finally broken her way through and had run off, howling, searching for Philip – not that Philip could have known – and the nights had become colder once there was no good reason to close the barn any more.

With the first trundling of the thunder, the rain began to fall in heavy drops, and when Andrew next looked at the slit, the people in the yard were pushing an envelope beneath the kitchen door, covering their heads with their coats, running back towards the track. Beside him, Di's eyes were open. She was shivering as she crawled towards him, whining, curling back up in his lap.

The lightning made the barn seem cavernous. In the moments of the flash, the walls appeared to spread until the roof was the size of the sky. The rain grew stronger. The drops falling between the dislodged slates became streams, and Andrew and Di were driven into a hole at the back of the stack where they huddled together, whimpering and waiting. Away along the hillside, in the lambing shed, Andrew could see the four dogs, curled in a mass, as close to his father as they could get without being sent away. Across the yard, in the kitchen, his mother was bent over the Rayburn, rocking as ever, waiting for the knocking to resume, and Andrew started to rock himself, at the thought of her, his eyes closed, a certain comfort in this thing that remained under his control.

Andrew knew about howling. He could tell a howl of loneliness from a howl of hunger, a howl to the moon from a howl in the face of a storm. It was the storm that howled, that was one thing. You yourself were just blank – as staring at circles in puddles was blank, or spinning down hillsides was blank – as the best and the greatest things in Andrew's life were always blank, and Andrew had even crawled blankly the whole way over the hill, where he had woken to find sheep that span in the air, where there were colours and lightness, where people had liked his father's tractor, where people had even liked the mirror that his hand was clamped to so tight in his pocket that you'd have had to have broken his fingers to take it away from him.

\* \* \*

The morning after the thunderstorm was Easter Sunday, and the world woke clean and shiny – seemingly amazed that it had made it through this cataclysm of fire and water, only to emerge on a more or less normal day. Across

Penllan, the grass had become fluorescent, as had the small yellow flowers that glowed amongst it, as had the primroses in the hedges and the full-blown leaves of the chestnut trees. It was as if everything was revealing more of itself on mornings like these – whether from shock, or relief, or exaltation – or as if you were yourself able to see a little wider, to glimpse in this sudden beauty something of the world's subliminal extent.

In the barns, coloured eggs appeared beneath the bantams, and Robin and Martin set out before breakfast to comb through the haylofts, searching the spaces between bales, the holes in the walls, the places in the rusted-up workings of ancient machinery. They scrambled up pillars, shouting as they spotted a speck of blue amongst a mass of brooding feathers, a flower-shaped arrangement of eggs on the top of the highest stack. They waved their arms to drive off the hens, gathering their eggs in a hay-lined basket while the cocks crowed and preened and ignored them along the beams.

Dropped in boiling water, the eggs began to shed their colours instantly – green, blue, yellow, red, rising in plumes, fanning as they came to the surface, remaining beautiful for a moment or two as the colours swirled together. Then the saucepan turned to a brownish murk and you couldn't see anything at all, until, five minutes later, Tara sat regular eggs on the table and cracked the tops with a teaspoon.

The ordinariness of the eggs, Tara explained as she chopped up their toast into soldiers, was entirely to be expected. Coloured eggs were, of course, magic – deposited in the barns during the night by the egg fairy, who was the tooth fairy for the rest of the year. Her eggs were entirely harmless, just so long as you could make them vanish again by noon of the next day. This meant, first, that you had to boil off the colour, then you had to eat them, making sure that you didn't leave even the tiniest scrap, then you had to throw the shells on the compost heap with a particular incantation.

If you did all of these things correctly, then you were allowed to eat some chocolate: the only time that you were allowed to eat chocolate in the entire year. And if you didn't, then the egg would hatch and grow into a chicken the same colour as its egg all over, very angry and larger than the house.

* * *

After breakfast, Tara and the two boys set off towards the ruined cottage, holding hands until they had to climb the gate beneath the chestnut tree, where it became a bit too complicated. Tara had a number of thin metal stakes beneath one arm and a tape measure clipped to her jeans. As they were crossing the field, she sang them a nursery rhyme in French – all about standing in the moonlight – but when she tried to teach it to them they all started giggling and the boys had still only managed to learn the first line by the time that they arrived.

Fine threads of grass were growing from the scar of the old track to Werndunvan, the earth dark from the recent rain. Down the hill, beside the water trough in the boundary hedge, there were the twisted remains of a giant bonfire whose diesel-ridden smoke had made Penllan all but uninhabitable a few nights earlier.

"Okay," said Tara, and consulted a piece of paper. "We need to measure out the garden, okay? So, Robbo, if you could stand next to the gatepost a moment, and Mart, you come with me and stop where I tell you."

"Why are we measuring Andrew's cottage?" asked Robin.

"Robbo," said Tara. She positioned Martin at the end of a piece of string, just beyond the damson trees. "Robbo, I've been trying to explain to you. This isn't Andrew's cottage any more. We've bought it."

"Why?" Robin asked.

"We're going to rebuild it," Tara explained. "So that people can come here for their holidays."

"Oh," said Robin, frowning.

Robin had never been particularly interested in the ruined cottage before – strangely, considering that he had, at various times, been fascinated by everything from an old water tank up on Cold Winter to the slits in the walls of the haylofts, which were obviously arrow slits, which meant that the barn had obviously once been a castle, and had dungeons still beneath it, piled high with treasure. It was something to do with the cottage's missing front wall. It defused its mystery – the same way that even Martin found it hard to get excited about a skull without a face. You needed features to get your thoughts started, details, things for your mind to lock onto.

But, looking again at the cottage, Robin was pleased to find that he owned it. At least, if they found treasure there, then he would be able to keep it. And it did have a bread oven, which he had once managed to squeeze himself into. And then there was the fireplace with the metal grille, whose chimney you could look up and see the sky in a fat black frame.

"What would you think about going round to play at Andrew's sometime?" said Tara, writing down a number in her notebook.

"When?" asked Robin.

"Whenever you like," said Tara.

Martin looked suspicious.

"Well, you have a think about it," said Tara. "Andrew's a nice boy, and he's got that new puppy, hasn't he? Di... You might have fun."

She tapped one of the stakes into the ground, next to Martin's feet, and let the tape measure suck back into itself.

"Tara?" said Martin, after a moment, still holding his piece of string. "Tara, can we have a story now?"

"A story about when you were at school!" said Robin.

"Yeah!" Martin agreed.

Tara scribbled down two more numbers in her notebook, which she then turned into a complicated-looking sum, murmuring under her breath. She took the end of the piece of string from Martin, tied it to the stake, and rubbed her forehead.

"School?" she said. "Wouldn't you rather hear about something happy?"

"Like what?" asked Martin.

"Like..."

"Like, when you found Ty'n-y-coed!" said Robin.

"Ty'n-y-coed!"

"Ty'n-y-coed!" Martin echoed.

"Okay, okay!" Tara laughed and sat down on one of the pieces of rubble that the cottage had instead of a front wall. She leant forward and peered through the gate towards the house to see if anyone was coming, then wrinkled her forehead in the way that she always did when she was about to begin a story. "Now, then. Well... Not long after Layla and I got back from India, I had nowhere to live. So," she rolled her eyes, "I had to go and live with my father..."

"Why did you just do that with your eyes?" asked Robin.

"Robin!" said Martin. "You're stopping the story!"

"Oh, your grandfather," said Tara. "You know what he's like."

Robin did know what their grandfather was like: a kind old man who looked extraordinarily like Tara, and who supplied them with chocolate from time to time when she wasn't looking. There was a portrait of him in the hall in which he looked rather different – in fact, he looked strict and horrible, like he was about to shout at you – but the portrait and their grandfather were not at all the same thing. Their grandfather played cricket with them and told them stories about when he used to fly an aeroplane, and Robin loved it when he came to visit – even if it always made Tara cross.

The two boys watched as she tapped her feet against a stone. "If your grandfather had his way," she continued, "I would probably be a scientist in a city somewhere. Or rather, I would probably be married to a scientist..."

"What about us?" asked Martin.

"You two would probably get packed off to boarding school," said Tara.

"You were packed off to boarding school," said Robin.

"Exactly," said Tara. She paused. "You see, to your grandfather, the world is in black and white. If he had his way, you two would be learning reading, writing and arithmetic. Nothing else. No castles, no astronomy. He wouldn't like Mr Gwynne at all."

"You like Mr Gwynne, don't you, Tara?" asked Robin.

"Of course," said Tara. Her feet paused, then resumed their tapping on the stone. "I think Mr Gwynne is wonderful. He's an excellent teacher."

"I like Mr Gwynne," said Robin.

"Good," said Tara, and breathed deeply. "I'm very glad you do. You see, the thing about your grandfather is that he only thinks, he doesn't feel... Do you understand what I mean?"

Robin nodded, not because he did, but because he could always tell when his mother was getting upset and he always did whatever he thought might make her feel better again.

Tara became upset whenever she talked about their grandfather, and Robin always burnt with questions on the subject, if only because the whole thing was such a mystery. His mother was right, of course – that went without saying – but then surely his grandfather ought to have been right as well. Sometimes Robin had a feeling like there was some great obstacle in between them – like the black empty space between two planets. Whichever way he looked at it, you were never allowed to be friends with them both at the same time.

\* \* \*

The story was all about Ty'n-y-coed, the cottage where Tara and Adam had lived when they first arrived in Radnorshire, where they had learnt to farm, years and years into the past. Robin didn't like to think of his parents as living in a cottage – they lived in a house – but a cottage it had been, and a humble one at that: without a track or running water, a telephone or even any electricity until Adam had exchanged their Volkswagen for the old Ferguson tractor and had connected it to a plug so that the record player worked when their friends came to visit and they could put coloured lights on the tree on Christmas Day.

The cottage had consisted of five small rooms, with a couple of deteriorating barns across the yard. Nobody had lived there since the days of old Miss Powell, who had been no further than the nearest village in sixty years. As a girl, Miss Powell had been a maid in the house of Lord Powys, but she had fallen pregnant not long after her sixteenth birthday and been sent away in disgrace. Lord

Powys had scoured his maps for the most obscure piece of property in his possession, and here he had built her a cottage and a couple of neat little barns, where she had been left to get on with it.

Robin already knew almost everything there was to know about Ty'n-y-coed, but he still loved to hear about it more than anything. Tara told them about how she and Adam had turned off the road to Llanddewi-Brefi, where they had been going to see Layla, because it had been such a beautiful day that they hadn't been able to sit in the car another minute. She told them about how they had wound up a lane between the auburn hillsides and then set off up through the heather, stopping occasionally to look back across the parallel waves of the hills, towards the wall of the Black Mountains that marked the edge of Breconshire.

Ty'n-y-coed they had found quite by chance, as they were dropping back down from the hilltop, following a path around an outburst of rock into a crowd of ragged trees. Suddenly they were standing at a gate between a cottage and a pair of old barns, between the cultivated farmland and the open hills. Beneath them, the ground fell away into a deep, steep valley, where a red-leaved wood surrounded a stream and tiny fields spilt upwards from a squat-looking farmhouse – a farmer crossing the yard between the barns, his sheepdog padding behind him.

Tara and Adam set out to explore the cottage at once, scattering sheep in the scullery, climbing the stairs to poke around the bedrooms, fiddling with the range to see if it could be persuaded back into life, disturbing a barn owl in the barns and sending it flapping away into the nearby trees. This was the time when Tara had just stormed out of her father's house and was planning to find a place of her own near Layla's, when Adam had a beard and was dreaming of becoming a farmer. The two of them had scarcely been at Ty'n-y-coed for ten minutes before they were marching down the hill towards the farmhouse, holding hands, watching the farmer who was now in one of the nearby fields, whistling and shouting, directing his dog around the sheep.

As Tara had explained on several occasions, this was Radnorshire proper – poor, poor ground, so thin and stony that several of the fields bordering onto the common land had been all but abandoned, the hedges having unravelled themselves into individual trees and the bracken having spilt through the holes into the wiry, sheep-trimmed grass. In the surrounding hills, there were people who saw omens in the approaching clouds, who refused to cut the hay around standing stones, who insisted that the wood of any tree struck by lightning would never burn, and that the hills were thick with the ghosts of the unfortunate souls who had drowned up in the mawn pools – the old peat cuttings, whose banks floated treacherously on the deep, brown water.

Owen, the farmer, however, was not of this type. He turned his head as they approached, his body stooped over his stick like it was still intent on the sheep that his dog was shuffling through a gateway. He was a small, wiry figure, with mismatched wellies and a magnificent pair of white sideburns that obscured most of his face. As it turned out, he had been champion of the Radnorshire sheepdog trials on three separate occasions – he had even competed in America and Australia – but on this occasion he seemed strange and suspicious, his eyes moving from Tara's hair, to the colourful print on Adam's T-shirt, to the mud on their wide-bottomed trousers.

"Been up Ty'n-y-coed, have you?" he asked.

"Er..." said Tara. "The cottage?"

"Ar," Owen nodded.

"Yes," said Adam. "Um... We're sorry to bother you, but do you happen to know who owns it?"

"That'd be me," said Owen, glancing back at his sheep, which the collie had now trapped against the hedge, awaiting further instructions.

"Oh," said Tara. "It's just that, it didn't look as if there's anybody living up there, and we were thinking that, well... perhaps you might be prepared to rent it out?"

"Rent?" Owen frowned. "Oh... No, no, I couldn't rent him out. No... No, if you two wants to go and live up there, that's your own business, but I ain't getting no money from him as he is, look, so I can't very well just go and take it off you now, can I?"

"Oh," said Tara. "Great."

"Thank you," said Adam.

"Don't thank me," said Owen, warming slightly. "I ain't done nothing. It'd be good to have someone up there, anyhow, put a bit of life back in the old place..."

"Perhaps," Adam suggested tentatively. "If you won't accept any rent, perhaps we might be able to, you know, give you a bit of a hand about the place instead, from time to time..."

Owen took a pipe from his pocket, blew down it sharply and nodded a few times.

"Ar," he said eventually. "That ain't such a bad idea. Just while I'm off at the trials, look, or if I'm doing a bit of fencing... Come to that, it never hurts round lambing time neither." He stroked his sideburns, then smiled to himself and whistled to his dog. "Well... I 'spect I'd best show you round, then, hadn't I?"

# CHAPTER SEVEN

# THE PRINCES

Werndunvan wasn't a tidy farm like Penllan. The hedges and fences were full of holes, and the sheep were thin and seemed to look at Robin sideways as he swung open the gate at the end of the track, pretending not to swing on it. To the left was the forestry, which enclosed a whole side of the farm like a pair of jaws. It flickered as the car moved off again, the dark lines of pines revealing endless, lifeless tunnels between them, vanishing away towards the stream.

But there were lambs in the fields, too, hurtling in packs amongst the scars of the bulldozer. There were hawthorns coming into blossom up on the hillside. There were swallows who had been all the way to Africa and were now swooping out above the valley, intercepting insects, working furiously at nests in the eaves of some barn or another, shuffling at the edges of puddles, gathering up the mud.

"Okay, Mart?" said Tara, as they rolled up into the yard. "There's nothing to worry about, okay? I'll stay and drink tea in the kitchen. We'll be here for an hour or so, that's all..."

She stopped the car and pulled on the handbrake, while Robin looked back over his shoulder, past the bottom of the yard, through the frame of a new shed, at the great bare hills of Wales, bulging into the sky as the black-grey clouds bulged down towards the earth. The farmhouse was imposing in the way of a particularly good skull. Its walls were more or less intact, but there were patches of corrugated iron on its face and its roof, cracks and holes, and the empty window sockets had been repaired only with fertiliser bags which were now in tatters, their writing and original colours all but bleached away.

Not that any of this was exceptional. At Llanoley, one of the barns had fallen down altogether and the cattle waded belly-deep in manure. At the Allt - up towards Ty'n-y-coed - there wasn't a piece of glass left in the place, and the Hughes boys hadn't spoken a word to one another in twenty-five years.

Tara had to knock three times on the kitchen door before there was any sign of movement inside. Robin and Martin stood behind her, Martin clinging to the leg of her trousers while Robin remained near the gate, trying to look independent. He watched the dark shape growing through the frosted glass, the handle as it flopped up and down before the door came open.

"Morning, Dora," said Tara, brightly. "How are things? I've just brought the boys round to play..."

Dora's eyes turned slowly from them to the barns, while Tara tapped her hands on the hips of her jeans – her back pockets embroidered with birds whose tails were long and glorious.

"Is Andrew about?" Tara smiled, without much success. "Perhaps we could shout for him? He's not in the kitchen, is he?"

Abruptly, Dora lumbered past them and set off into the yard, stepping through the mud and the puddles. Robin glanced at Martin, who was still hanging onto Tara's leg, sucking his thumb, apparently beginning to panic. He looked at the barns, and was cheered to find that they had arrow-slits of their own in the haylofts, which meant that they probably had dungeons, too, with treasure in aisles and piles.

"Andrew!" called Dora in her low, expressionless voice. "Andrew!" Across the valley, there was a shower coming on. The black clouds were sliding across the hills, the grey blear beneath them enveloping first the rust-coloured common land, then the fields with their miniature sheep, the Glyn and Llanshiver, ponds and orchards, woods and hedges.

"Andrew!" called Dora. "Andrew!"

"Hello, Andrew!" said Tara, as Andrew crept finally around the post of the barn door, his puppy bounding ahead of him and his left hand sunk into the pocket of his jacket.

Andrew glanced at her, then at Robin, who was still trying to maintain his independence, and for a moment it looked as if he was about to smile. But then he appeared to remember himself, and he turned his eyes back down to the dogs and the ground.

"I thought, perhaps," said Tara to Dora, her hand resting on Martin's head, "that I could come in for a cup of tea, let the boys get on with it for a while?"

A shiver of alarm crossed Dora's blank, white face, and she glanced up the hill towards the brown smear where there had once been a track to Penllan.

"No, no," she stammered. "No, no, he won't like... No, you can't..."

"Okay," said Tara. "Okay." She looked down at Martin, then over at Robin. "That's okay... Er..." She brushed some hair from her face. "What do you think then, Robbo? You're big enough to stay here for an hour or so, aren't you? Just while Martin and I go and do a bit of shopping..."

\* \* \*

It began to rain more or less as Tara and Martin drove away, and the dogs pursued them off along the track, barking and reaching for the wheels with their claws and their teeth. Robin was wearing a coat, so he did up the buttons and put up the hood, looked at Dora and waited for something to happen. Water ran through Dora's thin, grey-black hair, down into her grimy black dress. She gaped at the chewed-up mess of mud and grass, the concrete and stray stones of the yard, then she shivered and turned around, blinking sporadically.

"Boys," she said. "Boys, you best come in the house, you best... You... You... Chocolate, boys! You best have some chocolate!"

She trod heavily back towards the open front door, through the frenzy of circles in the puddles, and Robin glanced at Andrew, unsure whether or not this was a trick. But Andrew hurried straight after her, his puppy gathered up in his arms, so Robin decided to do the same.

The smell in the kitchen was overwhelming: somewhere between overcooked food and dog shit, sweat and decaying flesh. Robin paused a few steps inside, holding his nose despite himself. The table, the floor, the sink, the plates and cutlery, the windows and the walls, everything was encrusted in filth. The wallpaper dripped from the steam that was spewing from half a dozen pots on the Rayburn. It blossomed with moulds of strange and nameless colours.

"Mars bar," said Dora, retrieving a tupperware box from the top of the television, which was showing a cartoon. She removed two, replaced the lid and put the box back in its place, then she handed one to Robin and one to Andrew, and shuffled over to the Rayburn, where she set about raising and lowering the lids of the pots, poking at them with a long-handled wooden spoon.

Removing his fingers gingerly from his nostrils, Robin found that the smell was not as unbearable as he had at first thought. He climbed up onto a nearby chair, where he took the perforations of the black plastic wrapper carefully between two fingers, prising them apart to expose a corner of molten chocolate. This he took between his teeth, biting off a small chunk, which he allowed to dissolve on his tongue as he turned towards the television.

The cartoon was set in a narrow street, with walls to either side of it as tall and as featureless as cliffs. Standing on a collection of barrels and boxes, an army of red, pink, green and yellow cats were drumming on dustbins, tapping on bottles and strumming on tennis rackets – all of them wearing hats, scarves, jumpers, coats and waistcoats. But then a man who looked like one of the Sheenah, with a blue uniform and a peaked hat, came along and they all had to run away, chasing up clattering staircases and sliding down washing lines until they came to a huge abandoned barn next to a river full of tooting ships with smoke rising in puffs from their funnels. And inside the barn was a pile of treasure so big you could hardly have climbed to the top of it! There were crowns and necklaces, rubies and emeralds, and they were about to collect it all up and carry it away when a stupid little fat blue cat sneezed so hard that the entire barn fell down around them, and they had to go back to playing music instead.

\* \* \*

Even once the music had stopped and the screen showed only a long list of names, Robin continued to grin at it, formulating things that he could say once he got back to school – distorting the story until there were tractors involved, and tanks, and the barn hadn't just fallen down, it had been blown up by an enormous bomb with little fins on the back.

When Robin looked round him again, the first thing he noticed was that Andrew was watching him from under the peak of his cap, his jaw shivering as if he was about to say something. Di was rolling in the filth beside him, occasionally attacking his boot. Dora was still bent over the Rayburn, stirring one of the pots with a circular motion, staring into the chimney breast.

"Robin?" said Andrew, at last. He jabbed his finger at the wall behind him. "You want... You want to see, then? You... You want to see where he were?"

Robin hadn't thought much about the little black mirror since the three of them had been spinning, although he knew at once what Andrew was talking about. The mirror intrigued him like the drawing-room at home intrigued him. Their living-room might have been all bright and airy, with toys and plants, but the drawing-room was for the grown-ups, who could do what they liked, who understood things, and the grown-ups chose the television, the thick green curtains, the room that was dark and mysterious.

Out in the yard, the shower had almost stopped now and the puddles were overflowing into one another, trickling along well-worn routes towards the cliff above the new shed. Andrew led him past a disused front gate, past a thin strip of dead weeds and brambles which had once been a lawn, around the corner of the house to a small door with moss in its cracks. It had a latch near the top, which Andrew flicked deftly with a stick that was leaning against the wall, so that the door swung open without him even having to push it.

"'Ere," he mumbled, bending down to stroke Di, whom he left on the doorstep, scratching at a missing chunk of hair on her flank. "It's... It's down 'ere, it is." The two of them were standing in an abandoned hallway with the feel of age and dampness in the air. To the left was a room containing a mouldering bed, while just in front of them was a flight of dangerous-looking stairs with bits of stone and plaster forming a kind of stream-bed all the way down it. Light was spilling between the banisters, but Andrew led the way right into a dingy passageway, past a couple of paintings and some kind of living-room full of velvet and mould-covered chairs, boxes spilling rotten clothes, bits of old curtains, books and crockery.

"Andrew?" said Robin, trying to make his voice sound as fearless as Andrew appeared. "Don't you ever get a bit scared, coming in here on your own? Aren't you afraid that it might be haunted?"

"Haunted?" echoed Andrew.

They had stopped at a large, panelled door, which had a handle of the type that you could reach. Through another door to the left, through a broken window, Robin could see out to the garden on the far side of the house, where trees of species that he had never seen before coiled together, sprouting dark, fleshy leaves and the buds of fat, white flowers.

"You mean, you don't know about ghosts?"

"Ghosts?"

"Ghosts!" said Robin, trying to speak with authority,

even if they were in a dark and obviously beghosted passage. "Ghosts are when... Ghosts are when people die, but they stay behind as ghosts and they haunt places. You see them all over the place! Ghosts are white and kind of see-through, and they're very, very scary! They do horrible things! They want to kill people!"

Andrew glanced at him and, for a moment, he looked a little nervous himself, shuffling from foot to foot, one hand still buried in his pocket. But then some other idea seemed to occur to him since he began to murmur a tune from the cartoon that they'd just been watching and turned back around towards the door.

The door opened into a room so big that it might have belonged to a giant: some immense ogre who would shortly come bursting through one of the other doors and start demanding the return of his magic chicken or carrying them off to become pets of the Queen of Brobdingnag. But the room's thick dust showed no signs of enormous feet, with or without claws, and there was light from a pair of large, dirty windows, so you could at least look out onto the yard of the regular Werndunvan.

In the exact middle of the ceiling was a vast chandelier, so impressive that it made everything else in the room look a bit mundane for a moment: a piano, a number of bits of furniture covered with sheets, a small black fireplace, a set of shelves lined with old books, a grandfather clock with a round white face. Then Robin noticed an area of the floor which was for some reason meticulously clean, like a window through the filth, and he realised that the chandelier and the room itself were of a piece.

He crouched down to look at the pattern on the floor, following its swarming with his eyes, trying to work out how you might put together such a mind-boggling jigsaw puzzle. "'Ere!" said Andrew, his left hand moving visibly in his pocket, his right hand pointing at the floor. "'Ere, he was! D... Down 'ere!"

"What? Just lying on the floor?" asked Robin.

"Ar," Andrew nodded. "I got... I got others, mind! I got other things!"

He went to a corner, where he moved aside a heap of ancient newspapers, revealing a large magnifying glass, a hairbrush with half of the bristles missing, a comb, a fountain pen and a pair of pince-nez without the lenses.

"Treasure!" Robin breathed. He picked up the objects one after the other, turning them over in his hands. "These could be priceless! This could be the comb of... of... Pwyll, Prince of Dyfed! You could be a missing Welsh prince, Andy, hidden away as a baby so your... your evil uncle wouldn't find you, and this comb could be the only way your old nurse will remember who you are!"

He looked at him excitedly.

"Ar!" cried Andrew. He picked up the pince-nez. "An'... An'..."

"Yes!" said Robin. "Her glasses! That's her glasses! And we need this magnifying glass, so we can find clues, so we can lock your evil uncle up in the barn!"

Looking up, Robin could see thrones suddenly in the sheet-covered chairs, gold in the murky colours of the wallpaper, jewels in the drops of the chandelier. "It's a palace!" he exclaimed. "Look, it's a real, proper palace!"

He grabbed a couple of newspapers from the heap in front of him and rolled them up as tightly as he could, handing one to Andrew and swinging his sword through the air. Through the windows, coiling plants had surrounded the house and giant ferns waved tropically in the sunshine. You could almost hear the roar of wild beasts far off into the forest, but no wild beast would have dared approach the palace of Robin and Andrew: the fairest palace that man had ever seen, many-coloured and covered in gold and precious stones. Prince Robin and Prince Andrew were the noblest and the most valiant of princes, and they had a fair dog named Diana who guarded them day and night, and together they overthrew the Sheenah, and they slew the evil uncle, and it was they who brought peace and contentment to this Island of the Mighty!

* * *

Sitting high up on the haystack, not far from the top of the bale elevator, Robin looked into the little black mirror and made a picture from the arrow-slits in the thick stone wall behind him. The slits commanded views far off into Wales – a place, in the reflection, which might have been the shadowy world of Mr Gwynne's stories, where dragons paced among the mountains and ruins dripped from the cliffs. Turning the mirror slowly, Robin inspected hills the colour of clouds, trees the size of toys, and he began to wonder if this hayloft might come in useful at some point – as a fortress in the war against the Sheenah.

"We can build battlements," he said thoughtfully, waving his legs off the edge of the stack. "All we have to do is stand up bales in a line."

"The... The Sheenah!" said Andrew.

"Exactly," said Robin. "And if they try to climb up the elevator, then we can push it over, so they all die!"

He looked past his feet down the great wall of bales, imagining his enemies as they plummeted, spinning and screaming, to smash their heads on the hard earth floor.

On the bales beside them, Di was scratching again at her bald patch. Around them, the chickens were complaining to one another, brooding on their eggs or strutting over the topmost bales. Far below them, Dora had appeared and was looking up at them with her featureless face, and if you listened very closely you could hear her low, monotonous voice:

"Boys! Come down, boys!"

Andrew had a finger in his mouth when Robin put the mirror down, and he looked at him with interest.

"Have you got a wobbly tooth?" he asked.

Andrew frowned, and glanced at his mother.

"I have," said Robin, wobbling his own. He flicked at some hay and sent it spiralling away through the air.

Regardless of Dora, Robin felt absolutely no compulsion to do anything at all. Werndunvan was a marvellous place, so far as he could tell, and the only thing that mystified him about it all was why Tara had been so enthusiastic for him to come here in the first place, given that it was full of all the things that he wasn't supposed to do. It seemed very clear to him now that any time he disliked anything at home, he would simply run away and come here, where he would be able to stay until his parents became nice to him again.

Such were his thoughts as the sounds of a car appeared distantly on the track, growing louder through one slit after another.

"Boys!" Dora continued. "Come down, boys!"

Tara stood with Martin in the doorway and looked from Dora, up to the two of them sitting at the edge of the hayloft, to the towering elevator that they had recently scaled with its shaky limbs and its regular knife-like blades. A frown-mark like Robin had never seen before cut between her eyebrows and up into her forehead.

"Robin, what the fuck do you think you're doing?!" she shouted, her voice shrill inside the heavy stone roof. "You two boys, get down from there this instant!"

# CHAPTER EIGHT

# INTO THE
# DANGEROUS WORLD

Spring always flushed Andrew with excitement. It was the time of warmth and safety – even in the early mornings, when the shadow of Cold Winter still curved out across the valley, the sky laced with thin clouds shining in the light of the arriving sun. Across the farm, the fields were covered with dandelions in clusters and constellations. Bluebells poured through the woods, and blossom burst from the hedges. They made Andrew want to laugh, to roll in the grass, to slither on his belly and chase the fat lambs across the hillside.

Yet the spring this year had brought as much punishment as joy. Twice his father had called him to sit beside him in the car, and had driven him through the village and away along the valley to a place called Abberton, glaring through the windscreen and cursing other drivers.

Here, among the milling, nameless people, he had ordered Andrew into shops, where he had bought him the red shirt with the lines that went upwards and sideways, the itchy grey trousers and the stiff brown shoes that squashed and hurt his feet. He had taken him into a shop that smelt of wax and oil, where a man in an apron had shorn the back of his head and made a straight line of hair above his eyes. For fully fifteen minutes, Andrew had sat in front of a mirror, squeezing his eyes shut against the reflection.

That morning, when his father called for him, the dogs abandoned their patch of sunlight and slunk away nervously into the barn. Philip got into the car and leant across to shove open the passenger door, so Andrew climbed up next to him. But even as they began to drive off, only Meg reappeared to watch them, her face lowered and her tail pressed between her legs.

"Where... Now where, Dad?" asked Andrew.

"School," spat Philip.

There was a pause.

"Ain't never been to school," said Andrew.

"That's right," said Philip. "And if I had anything to do with it, you wouldn't be fucking going now, neither. School never did me no fucking good. It won't do you no fucking good, you mark my words."

"Is Robin... Robin at school?" asked Andrew.

"Ar," said Philip, looking away from him towards the long-tailed lambs racing around the fields.

The car rolled down the hill towards the village, between the hedges, past the outlying cottages and the spire of the church poking above the yew trees. They passed the pub with its dark latticed windows and its hunched white walls, and if Andrew had been wearing his jacket he would have pulled it over his head so he didn't have to look at it all.

"Here you are," said Philip abruptly, as they stopped among a flurry of cars, in the long thin shadow that lay beside Offa's Bank. "Out you get, then. Go on..." He leant across Andrew to push open the door. "Go on, boy! I ain't got all day! Out you get!"

\* \* \*

Andrew stood on the pavement outside the school gates, and looked around him for something familiar. His trousers itched and his shoes cut into his feet. His collar squeezed his neck so that it was hard for him to breathe, and he would have turned and run directly back over the hill again, if only he had known which way to go, if only he hadn't been so terrified.

The gateposts were tall and spike-topped, and behind them there was a yard covered in jumbled lines of different colours, and behind that there was the red-brown building where he had once seen dozens of children, turning grey as you looked higher, then white where the roof came to a point in the pale blue sky. In the yard, a crowd of people was watching him, talking to one another. Andrew tried to look away from them, down towards his armpit, but the collar dug into his neck and his breathing became even more painful, and the only thing that he could think to do was to close his eyes and imagine that none of them were there at all.

"How long has he been here?"

When Andrew tipped his head back and sniffed at the air, he could smell the sheep and the lambs in the nearby fields. He could smell the dew on the grass, the sunlight spreading across the valley. He could even smell Werndunvan faintly – the warmth of the kitchen, the dogs, and the pots on the Rayburn – and the smell made him think about the time when there had been only Meg, the rain and the circles in the puddles, the smells of hay and damp stone. And somewhere far beneath all of these, he remembered his mother in the dingle beside the house, before her face had lost its detail, before it had started to rain, when the sunlight still filtered down between the trees.

"Andrew?" Someone was wiping at his cheeks. "Andrew, it's okay... Come on now, don't cry. Everything's okay. You're just in the wrong place, that's all."

Andrew peeped out the tiniest amount possible, but his eyes were all bleary from crying and he could see only mixed-up colours, white and blue and yellow. Then he realised that it was Tara speaking, kindly again, although she had shouted at him in the barn with Robin. He opened his eyes a little bit further so that he could see the gateposts, her sun-coloured hair and her eyes smiling down at him.

"It's okay, Andrew," she was saying, her voice calm and soothing. "It's okay. Don't cry now. You'll get your smart new clothes all wet... They're lovely clothes, Andrew! You look really good. Do you know that?"

Tara sat down on the step between the gateposts, smiling and patting the stone beside her, so he sat down as well.

"Come on now..." She wiped his cheek again with her white handkerchief. "That's it. There's nothing to be worried about. Nothing at all. Everything's going to be fine... Now, there's no hurry, okay? We can sit here just as long as you like... But, if you want to, the other boys and girls are just beginning to get ready for assembly. That's when everyone sits down together. They all sit down together in a lovely big room. They sing together and Mr Gwynne tells them a story. Robin will be there, and Martin, and Robin says that Mr Gwynne tells some wonderful stories. What do you think, eh? Would you like to come to assembly? You like stories, don't you?"

Andrew nodded, without thinking, and again he caught the smell of Werndunvan among the smells of the morning. Then Tara took his hand and he began to feel a bit better, and as they stood upright the gateposts were less tall than she was, and he did know some of the people in the crowd, after all – Maggie the Glyn, Mary Cwmithel, Jack from the council houses – and, however painful his feet, Andrew felt proud to be walking with Tara, in his new shoes, across the tangle of colourful lines.

Inside the school there were children everywhere, hurrying around carrying chairs or piles of books, and somewhere a long way above them – in the sky, as it seemed – a metallic clanking began, which reminded Andrew of his father nailing up sheets of corrugated iron. Along the wall in front of him there was a row of hooks, each of them accompanied by a picture: a tractor, an apple, a tree, and many other colourful things that Andrew had never seen before. Under one of these, a girl with blue-framed glasses was changing her shoes, her hair hanging over her face, and she was so grown-up that she had breasts bigger than Tara's.

"Hello, Andrew!" said a friendly sounding voice. "You are Andrew, aren't you?"

Andrew looked at the man who had spoken to him, then he looked at Tara to check that he was alright – her face a little redder suddenly, now that they were inside. The man was tall, with a wave of dark hair at the top of his forehead, and fine, precise hands – not like his father's at all. He was smiling, exchanging occasional comments with the boys and girls who pressed past them through the doorway into an enormous room flooded with the sunlight that was spilling now from the top of Offa's Bank.

"I'm very pleased you're here, Andrew," the man went on. "Tara's told me lots about you, and you're already friends with Robin and Martin, aren't you?"

"This is Mr Gwynne, Andrew," Tara explained. "He's going to be your teacher, so if you need anything you just ask him, okay?"

Andrew nodded and watched as a group of girls hurried past them, giggling and skipping up the stairs.

"Thankyou, Tara," said Mr Gwynne, quietly. "I don't think I've ever seen a first day quite... well, quite like this before."

"Well," Tara sighed. "We have had our fair share of experiences with Philip... I'm a bit surprised he brought him here at all, to be honest."

"I appreciate it, anyway," said Mr Gwynne. "And you're sure it's okay for Robin—?"

"I think so," said Tara. "We'll just have to play it by ear, Huw, but let's try it and see how it goes."

Andrew was beginning to feel more comfortable now, even excited. Through the doorway he caught a glimpse of white-blond hair and further pictures and colours on the walls. He spotted a square of stars which could have been cut from the sky. He saw swirls of reds and greens, oranges and yellows, paintings of people, houses, trees, dogs and tractors. If Tara said that everything would be alright, then it had to be alright, and even if Tara went away again, then Robin would still be here, wouldn't he?

"What do you think then, Andrew?" said Mr Gwynne, smiling again. "Do you want to come into assembly now? I've saved you a seat next to Robin."

* * *

There tended to be a calm after lambing. On a good year, the worst of it lasted for about six weeks, after which Adam came staggering out into the sunshine, blinking, with six weeks of beard and sleeplessness and a constant cough from the pipe still hanging out of the left-hand side of his mouth. Robin and Martin would watch this figure from the lawn where the weather had found them, watch it vanish upstairs, hear the pipes clank, the tank in the attic rush and groan, black water gush into the drain outside the kitchen window and – finally – their father would reappear from the back door in a T-shirt instead of his tattered coat and go and position himself on a gate, watching the grass and the lambs growing together.

In truth, of course, Adam did not spend anything like as much of May sitting on a gate as he did mucking out the sheds, fixing fences, shooting moles, vaccinating, detailing, drenching and castrating, cutting firewood to dry ready for winter, and rebuilding the ruined cottage. This was always the way, however much he might have claimed to need a holiday, but if one or other of the boys were able to locate him on a gate at this time of year, then he would invariably come up with something interesting to tell you.

Adam loved to talk about sheep. He would tell the boys how all of them had different characters, just like humans had, and how some of them were clever and some of them were stupid, and some were greedy, and others adventurous, or uptight, or solitary, and if you didn't believe him, then you should just sit there for a few years and watch them yourself. He'd tell them how everyone in the country would have been surrounded by sheep once upon a time, and how Christians would have seen the whole idea of being a flock quite differently to the way that most people saw it today. Or he'd tell them about the peewits tumbling endlessly over their nests in the bog and the bottom fields, about owls and curlews, badgers and pine martens. Most of which went straight over Robin's head, so he would simply lean on the gate beside his father, looking towards the red curve of Offa's Bank, where the first bowed heads of the bracken were just pushing up through the bodies of their forebears, and listen to the sound of his voice.

* * *

Every year, at about this time, Bill Llanoley would find himself with time on his hands and embark on a wholesale massacre of rabbits. For two or three days, he would charge around the hillsides, mostly by night, discharging his shotgun at fleeing white tails until either the mood had passed or he had a sufficient mountain of rabbit bodies to feel that the point had been made.

"Fucking rabbits!"

Once he'd calmed down again, Bill would then set out on a tour of the neighbouring farms, presenting people with rabbits, enjoying the cups of tea and glasses of beer that he was given, and generally spreading gossip until his supply of rabbits had been exhausted, at which point he would return to his mother and their ruined barn for another year of hard labour.

There was an orchard at Penllan, which consisted of a couple of apple trees and a pear tree, where Tara would hang a hammock in the summer if the weather looked like it might hold for more than a day or two. It was surrounded by a loop of the track and the vegetable garden, and it was here that Robin and Martin were sitting, learning how to whistle, when Bill appeared in his green Daihatsu.

"How do, boys?" he said, slowing down beside them, his red face grinning from the open window.

"Hello, Bill!" said Martin.

"Look, Bill!" said Robin. He jabbed his finger at his upper jaw. "Look, I've got a tooth missing!"

"You have and all!" said Bill, exposing another half-inch of gum and a blackened molar. "You'll make a farmer yet, I reckon... Either of you two boys fancy a rabbit?"

"Yeah!" said Martin.

Robin said nothing.

"He's dead, mind."

"I want a dead rabbit," said Martin. "I'm going to be a vet, and vets chop dead rabbits open."

"Oh ar?" said Bill. "Well, if you qualifies in the next day or two, I've got a heifer needs a bit of a look. Just if you've got a moment..."

Appearing in the gateway to the yard, Adam had the look on his face that he often had at this time of year, when his projects became more about enthusiasm than necessity. In his hands he had a claw hammer, a plastic carton full of nails and a piece of wood about two feet long. When he saw Bill, the only change in his expression was a slight dimpling in either cheek.

"Rabbit time again!" he said, leaning on the bonnet and inspecting the grey-brown body that Martin was now cradling in his arms.

"Rabbit time!" Bill greeted him.

"Got a few this year?" asked Adam.

"How do I chop him open?" Martin demanded.

"Why?" said Adam. "You going to cook him?"

"He's going to be a vet," said Bill. "He's coming round to have a look at my heifer."

"Mmm," said Adam. "There is an old dissection kit about the place somewhere. Remind me later on, Mart. You can help me cut him up, if you like."

"Touch of foul, I 'spect," said Bill.

"Tell you what," said Adam. "Let's say we put up another bar for Meredith, then I'll go up the kitchen and get Bill a cup of tea. What do you reckon, boys? You coming to see if Meredith's about?"

Meredith was the only ewe at Penllan with a name, and due to some pact with Adam she had been excused the normal rules of sheepliness and was allowed to do absolutely whatever she pleased. This consisted mainly of wandering around the valley, vaulting fences and communing with distant relatives and tups at the wrong times of year. Aside from her sporadic production of lambs, Meredith's sole task was to accompany the other ewes to Offa's Bank each July, where they would all be left to graze for a month or so – except for Meredith, who would race Adam and his tractor back across the valley to Penllan, and invariably beat him.

"The thing is," said Adam to Bill, as they were crossing the side-field across the track, "Meredith isn't your average ewe and you can't go round treating her like she is. She can get in and out of any field in the valley and she knows it, and you've kind of got to respect that."

"I had a ewe like that myself about twenty years back,"

said Bill. He looked at Robin and Martin. "You should have seen her, boys, I swear! She was famous in the village, she was! She used to jump out of her field, just like a kangaroo, and off she'd go, out over Offa's Bank! She'd get as far as the Derw sometimes, but she'd always be back for her tea!"

"A kanga-ewe?" said Adam, raising an eyebrow.

"A kanga-ewe!" echoed Robin, laughing delightedly, and Martin joined in a moment later.

The side-field was long but narrow, and on its far side there was a stile with nail holes all over the posts. When the four of them arrived, Adam put down the plastic carton in the grass and picked out a couple of six-inch nails, one of which he stuck like a pipe in the corner of his mouth. Around him, the grass was deep now, thick with daisies, just at the height when it was beginning to tickle your legs.

"Belief!" he said, and nailed one end of the piece of wood to the stile with a couple of quick strokes. "That's the thing! You see, Meredith believes that she can get in and out of this field, which she always enters and exits by precisely the same route." He hammered in the other nail and stood back, turning to the boys for approval. "Believe it or not, no matter how high I raise this bar, she still goes sailing clear over the bloody thing!"

\* \* \*

For much of that afternoon, Tara had been pushing a wheelbarrow backwards and forwards from the big shed to the garden, her radio dangling from one of the handles and her dungarees smeared with manure. Where Adam tended to get overexcited about animals at this time of year, Tara would get equally absorbed in her vegetables – as you might have expected from the only vegan sheep-farmer in the known world. Either she was weeding around the onions or planting out basil and coriander in her home-made cloche, sprinkling slug pellets or erecting a series of great bamboo constructions, which would later vanish beneath runner beans and become some of the best hiding places on the entire farm.

"Ah!" she said, as the four of them arrived back at the track. She was pushing the empty wheelbarrow, and it took her a moment to close the garden gate properly behind her, rearranging the chicken wire with her boot to make sure that it was rabbit-proof. "Still doing good deeds for gardeners, Bill?"

"Bloody slaughter, this year!" said Bill.

"I'm glad to hear it," said Tara.

"Look, Tara," said Martin. "This is Sir Belvedere!"

He presented her with the dead rabbit, which Tara did her best to admire.

"Oh, Adam," she said. "Emily Jones rang just now. Apparently there's an Indian theme at the party tonight. I don't suppose you remember what happened to that shirt that Owl brought back with him from Manali that time, do you? I couldn't find it up in the attic, and it'd be perfect for you..."

Adam frowned, tapping his hammer against the car-ton so the nails jangled.

"You are coming, aren't you?" she asked.

"Well..." he said. "I did tell Bill that I'd go over and give him a hand with his barn later on. Parts of it are becoming a bit of a death trap..."

"If you're busy, look—" Bill started.

"Well, I did say," said Adam. "Look, perhaps it's best if I just come over and pick you up later... We're just going to have a quick cup of tea now, okay? Then I'll go and see if I can't do anything about those bloody gutters."

Robin was watching as Adam and Bill continued up the hill – the muscles moving in waves beneath Adam's T-shirt, stretching his sleeves until they looked like they might burst. Beside him, Tara picked the wheelbarrow up again, but then she seemed to think better of it and put it back down, pulling off her gloves and rubbing her temples with her clean, white fingers, staring across the valley towards the invisible mark of the English border.

"Tara?" asked Robin. "Is it a Red Indians party?"

"No, Robin," said Tara, distantly. "It's an Indians from India party."

"Oh!" said Robin. "We're learning about Indians from India at school! 'Namaste!' That's what Mr Gwynne says."

"That's good," said Tara.

"Is Mr Gwynne going to be at the party?" said Robin.

"I expect so, yes," said Tara.

A few feet away, Martin had arranged the rabbit on his lap and was lifting up its ears, apparently trying to see into its brain. Robin had always hated dead animals and he could barely even look at it without thinking about the cold fur, the blackened holes of the shotgun pellets, the eyeballs staring blankly into the grass.

"Tara?" asked Robin. "What does sexy mean?"

"Why do you want to know that?" said Tara, frowning, turning from Offa's Bank and looking down at him.

"Well," said Robin, "Nigel told me that Gethin thinks you're sexy."

"Ah," said Tara.

She said nothing else for several seconds, and Robin began to worry that he might have somehow upset her. So he moved a bit closer and put his arms round her hips.

"Are you okay, Tara?" he asked eventually.

"Yes," said Tara. "Yes, I'm fine... It's just your father. He can be a bit difficult at times, that's all."

"Like grampa," said Robin, helpfully.

"Maybe a bit." Tara took her gloves from the side of the wheelbarrow and began to pull them back on. "I'd just have liked him to come along to the party, that's all... Well, Robbo, sexy means... If someone fancies someone else, if they want them to be their boyfriend or their girlfriend, then they think that they're sexy. But... I'm sure Gethin's very nice, but I don't really think that I want to be his girlfriend."

Robin laughed, but she hardly seemed to notice as she picked up the wheelbarrow and continued on her way to the big shed and its pile of straw and manure.

# CHAPTER NINE

# A Place of Ghosts

There was rarely a time at school when Andrew couldn't smell Werndunvan: the dogs, the bales, the kitchen where his mother clung to the front of the Rayburn. At different times he smelt different things, so one day he might smell Di at his desk beneath the room-wide windows, the mustiness of the bald, scratchy patches on her skin. But then he would smell Meg, and he would think about times when they had been curled up together in the hay, when she had kept him from the cold, licked the dirt from his face, whined to keep him company.

"Right," said Mr Gwynne across the room, frowning at the picture that he was drawing on the blackboard – the latest in a long line of odd-shaped beasts and birds. "This is an Indian elephant, which is the biggest animal in the entire country. Now, Indian elephants grow to about ten foot tall, so if you can imagine a large four-wheel-drive tractor – a Ford 4100, say – that's the kind of size that we're talking about..."

Andrew was hungry, and it was always next to impossible to think properly at this time of day. From the hatch to the canteen he could smell the first, maddening smells of dinner – roast lamb and potatoes, possibly with ice cream for sweet – and his mind was thick with carrots and gravy, chocolate sauce and crispy bits of fat. Mrs Garraway, the school cook, took her job very seriously. She was, as she put it, responsible for the future of the entire village, and as a result she bought only the very finest cuts of meat from the village abattoir – which happened to be run by her son, Jim – while she grew almost all of the vegetables herself, in the enormous garden behind her cottage.

Beneath the desk, Andrew polished the glass of his little mirror on a corner of his shirt, humming quietly to himself and stroking the cushion with the tips of his fingers. Checking that Mr Gwynne was busy with his picture of a large, stripy cat, he lifted it until it was higher than the windowsill, and looked out at the world behind him: the playground with its mysterious grids and spirals, the bungalows on the main road, the flat fields that flooded in the spring and the autumn, the farms converging as they rose towards the hilltop.

Andrew could see things in the foreground, too, although in the mirror they became darker and appeared to bulge towards him. Ranging along the windowsill were the animals that the class had made at the end of the previous term, caught in the midday sunlight, chicken wire welling from their wildly coloured sides. Turning the mirror a fraction, he could make out Robin, sitting at his desk next to Nigel and the Wendy house, intently copy- ing the cat onto the paper in front of him. Andrew was the only child in the class who sat alone at his desk, and above all he loved those days when Robin would come and sit beside him for a while and whisper to him about the Sheenah, about the caves inside Cold Winter and the adventures they would have in the untold weeks of the summer holidays.

"Andrew?" said Mr Gwynne abruptly, lowering his chalk and staring at him. "What on earth have you got there?"

Andrew froze, looking past the reflection, and it was a moment or two before he realised that Mr Gwynne was talking about his little mirror. Instantly, he felt a prickling sensation on the back of his head, the muscles twitching around his mouth, although it wasn't until Mr Gwynne began, cautiously, to move towards him that he managed to snatch the mirror away between his legs – where he would put his hands when he was lying at night in the barn – bending his head over on top of himself so that nobody could see his face, closing his eyes as tightly as possible and hunching his shoulders into his ears.

"Andrew," said Mr Gwynne, gently, his voice now almost beside him. "Come on, there's no need to be upset. I'm not cross with you..."

His face pressed into his arms, Andrew could smell the Werndunvan smells stronger than ever. In his mind, he was back in the hayloft, darting across the open bales with Di just behind him, sliding through a crack in the stack in the corner. Here was a cavity the exact size of a boy and his puppy, and Andrew murmured noises of comfort to her, nuzzling her neck as he scraped the strands of hay back across the entrance – trying to ignore Mr Gwynne, whose hand was now on his shoulder – restoring the wall of bales until you could have searched the barn forever and never have hoped to find them.

"Andrew, come on," said Mr Gwynne, and it sounded like he was smiling. "Let's make a deal, okay? You sit back up and show me whatever you were just playing with, and I promise that I won't take it away from you... Okay?" He paused, and Andrew could hear the giggles and whispers in the room around them. "Later on, I'm going to need someone to help me stick up everyone's pictures on the walls... What do you think, eh? Would you like to help me stick up pictures this afternoon?"

Without a thought, Andrew nodded, uncurling gradually until he was sitting back upright. He glanced at the faces staring at him from around the room, but still he reached between his legs and sat the little mirror on the desk in front of him.

"Good Lord," said Mr Gwynne, almost to himself.

He took the leather-covered case and held it up to the sunlight, shaking his head, turning it over several times before he unfastened the catch and inspected the cushion, the golden frame and the blackened curve of the glass. He turned his back to the window, lifted the mirror above his left shoulder and ran his eyes across the reflection, the stifled colours and the miniature events taking place on the hill beneath Wiggington.

"Well," said Mr Gwynne, as if there was no one in the room besides the two of them. "I don't know whether you know anything about this thing already, Andrew, but it's called a Claude glass. I've never actually seen one before, I've only read about them, but in the eighteenth century artists and tourists – that's people who like to go around looking at things – used to carry them around with them to look at the countryside. It was one of those funny things that they liked to do in those days, to make the world look like a picture... Where on earth did you get it?"

The other children were giggling less all of a sudden, and Andrew began to feel a little braver as his eyes flickered between the mirror and the face of his teacher.

"I found him," he said.

"Where?" asked Mr Gwynne. "Where did you find him?"

"In the big room," said Andrew.

Mr Gwynne smiled, running the end of his finger across the cushion that faced the mirror. He closed the catch and handed it back.

"Andrew's is a very interesting house," he told the class, moving a foot or two away from him, looking around the room. "Once upon a time, it used to belong to a man named Thomas Hutchinson, who was a farmer from the north of England. He was the brother-in-law of a very great poet called William Wordsworth. I'll tell you what – after lunch I'll read you all one of his poems."

\* \* \*

The rain fell softly outside the living-room. It hissed in the trees, hushed the sheep in the fields, tinkled in the guttering and popped in drops on the fertiliser bags beside the shed. Like the background fuzz of a record, it was a noise that you heard rather than listened to – creeping unnoticed into your consciousness, muted by the walls and the windows, lit by the colourless light of the early evening.

Robin sat at his table in the corner, beneath the tall brass lamp with the tassels on its lampshade, and his eyes were blurred as he stared at the lines and the figures that trailed away down the paper in front of him. Through the ceiling, he could just hear Martin and Oliver, his brother's best friend, plotting their assault on the Sheenah, discovering priest's holes and tunnels that bored into the heart of the hill. Through the door to the kitchen, he could hear his parents talking excitedly about something, and it was bad enough having to do addition, subtraction and times tables every evening without having to listen to everything that you were missing out on as well.

Ever since the end of lambing, Adam had made Robin do half an hour's homework every day after school – setting him maths exercises, and marking them promptly for the following morning. What he had done to deserve this treatment, Robin couldn't begin to imagine. At school, Mr Gwynne gave them extra work only by way of a punishment, and it seemed to Robin now that he had been punished every single day for a whole month. A month of misery, with no hope at all before the summer holidays!

"Look," said Tara, somewhere not far from the kitchen door. "I like Huw Gwynne, okay? I think he's a bloody good teacher."

"Yes, I know you do..." Adam paused. "And I'm sure he's got his strengths. But that's not really the issue, is it? Yes, he gets them enthused, but for what purpose? I mean, how are these children supposed to sit an exam when they can't write properly?"

There was a kind of growling noise, and Tara seemed to be stamping as she walked across the square, red tiles.

"You sound like my bloody father!" she said.

"Well, just this once, maybe I do," said Adam. "Maybe this time he wasn't being all that unreasonable."

"Of course he wasn't being bloody unreasonable!" Tara snapped. "He is never unreasonable, just as he is never understanding!"

The volume of their voices was coming and going, and for a time Robin could hear nothing but the odd syllable. He looked again at his horrible homework, cupped his hand around his ear, then – careful to be as quiet as possible – he stood up from his table and tiptoed over to the doorstep, where he sat back down again, leant towards the door, pulled his knees up to his chest and pushed his thumb into his mouth.

"They're bright kids, Tara," Adam was saying, calmly. "That's the point. I've no doubt at all that there's a lot of stimulation in... Welsh mythology and the future of the cosmos. But what happens in four or five years' time? What happens when they get to Abberton Comp? I mean, you look at Stuart, John the Glyn's son. He spent five years bunking off, sniffing glue behind the bus shelter. He's got nothing to show for it. Huw Gwynne... Huw Gwynne is a distraction. You must see that? It isn't going anywhere."

Tara sat a saucepan on the Aga with a clunk, and a second or two later there was a clicking noise as she cut up some vegetable or another on the chopping board. Leaning closer still towards the door, covering his left eye with his hand, Robin could make out a sliver of kitchen through the crack around the frame – a slice of the table where Adam was packing his pipe, a wider slice of the Aga where a saucepan was just coming to the boil, its steam bubbling upwards into the dense grey smoke of the tobacco.

"Look," said Tara, and her voice sounded taut. "We live on a Welsh hill farm, okay? The fact is, you live on a Welsh hill farm, you get Welsh hill-farm children. It's as simple as that... The boys are healthy, they've got space, they're surrounded by nature, they've got all of the bloody things that I never had when I was a kid and I'm absolutely buggered if I'm going to go and take it all away from them!"

"Yeah," said Adam, "but when it comes down to it, even Andrew's got most of that lot."

"Oh, don't be fatuous!" Tara spat.

"Who's being fatuous?" said Adam. "Tara, not a single child went from Abberton to university last year. Not one!"

It had occurred to Robin, as he struggled with his extra work, that he should do as he had told himself when he was at Werndunvan, and simply run away. Many times he had thought about the big, dusty room with its collection of treasures, about the hayloft, the Mars bars, the puppy and the television, but somehow there was something that held him back. Cold Winter seemed to have grown between the two farms, become ominous and insurmountable, and, since Tara wouldn't let him play there again, Werndunvan too seemed suddenly much scarier: a place of ghosts and floors that might collapse at any moment, where the wilderness didn't just stop at the doors and the windows but carried on through the rooms and the passageways, dissolving them piece by piece, sucking them away into the outside air.

Robin heard the splash as Tara dropped the vegetables into the boiling water, and as he peered again through the crack between the door and its frame his mother looked cornered. It was all that he could do not to come running to help her.

"The thing is," Adam continued, "we chose to live on a Welsh hill farm, Tara. It's a very significant distinction. We chose to go to university. We can't just deny our children the same choice that we had."

"Christ, Adam!" Tara turned round, glowering. "You're the bloody... zealot round here! You're the one who insists on playing the Radnorshire hill farmer! Adam Penllan! Don't make out like I'm the only one who wanted to bring them up here!"

"Could you stop being so emotional about it?"

"So what are you suggesting?"

"That we take up your father's offer," said Adam.

"There are other schools. Not near here, no, but there are other schools."

Upstairs, Martin and Oliver were bouncing on one of the beds. Robin could hear them quite clearly, although such was the hush of the dim, watery evening that he would never have thought that they could have been heard in the kitchen. He remained on the step, watching his mother and father glaring at one another across the warm red glow of the floor.

"They're too young," said Tara, quietly.

"Robin is seven and a half," said Adam.

"Exactly," said Tara.

"You were away at boarding school when you were his age, Tara!" said Adam. He paused to puff on his pipe. "Look, I don't want him to leave, either. But he would only need to be away four nights a week. He'd be back here every weekend..."

"What the fuck would you know about it?" Tara shouted. "What would you know about being sent away from your family when you're seven years old and dumped among strangers? The fucking... trauma of it! I will never, never, send my children away like that! Never!"

"So Robin gets the reverse?" asked Adam, his voice as stable as ever. "Even if it's just as bad... Tara, three of the other children in his class have been forbidden to talk to him by their mothers because he's giving them nightmares! This... Sheenah thing. I swear, he's so tied up in his imagination, I can't tell sometimes whether he knows what's real and what's not, and, frankly, it's not doing Martin any favours, either..."

"Do you even know where it comes from?" Tara interrupted. "Do you know what Sheenah means?"

There was a moment's silence. Robin put his hands to his ears, but he couldn't stop listening, watching the back of his father's head, clouds of smoke ballooning around it.

"Machines," said Tara. "It's bloody machines! That's where it comes from! Thanks to your bloody machines, Robin's convinced he's on the point of being attacked by some kind of mechanical army..."

"That's just ridiculous!" said Adam. "How are you supposed to run a farm without machinery?"

"So we need that huge blue truck of yours, do we?" said Tara, furiously. "And Philip needed to spend more than he's ever spent on his wife and his son in their entire fucking lives to get a stupid tractor and a stupid bulldozer just so he could compete with you?!"

Adam continued to smoke in his chair, light glancing from the crown of his head, his fingers drumming on the table in front of him.

"So," he said, eventually, "what about Hereford College?"

"The College is a private school," said Tara. "You know what I think about private schools. And, besides, we're completely fucking skint, in case you hadn't noticed."

She reappeared in the crack, drying her hands on her apron, and as she looked at Adam her face appeared to be trembling, the muscles shivering in her cheeks and around her eyes.

"Okay, okay," she said. "So my father wants to pay for Robin to leave his family and the school he loves..."

"Come on, Tara," said Adam. "I don't want him to go any more than you do – you know that – but we have got to be sensible about this..."

"No!" Tara turned and slammed something down hard on the sideboard. "No... I don't have to be sensible about this. Adam, there is a line to be drawn here! I'm not going to send them away!"

There was another long, horrible pause in which Robin bit his thumb so as not to make any noise.

"So what do you suggest, then?" asked Adam "We move? We sell the farm?"

# CHAPTER TEN

# THE TERRIBLE
# SUNLIGHT

With the start of June the rain stopped again, and this time it didn't return. The sheep crept out from under the trees, bald and scrawny - shorn with the first flush of sunshine and not so much bigger now than their fat, hairy lambs. Around them, the grass was beginning to straighten, fanning and filling the fields, discovering flowers, thistles and banks of nettles in the shade. Along the hedges and on the hillsides where the bracken was pushing in spears from the moist ground, the blossom ceased to be an aspect of the general greyness - like the sheep, like the flowers and the butterflies - and suddenly the hawthorn trees, the damsons and the crab apples were cascades of white in the hot sunlight.

Summer had, it seemed, been progressing all along, behind the lines of the rain and the low sullen clouds, in the elevated regions where the buzzards were once again spiralling, surveying their dominions: the shining streams and ponds teeming with tadpoles, the green-brown closeness of the hilltops, the twisting roads and dingles, and the woods where bluebells rippled like water and where there were orchids, if you knew where to look for them, or sheep if they had happened to get there first.

In the abandoned hallway at Werndunvan, sunlight came through cracks so tiny you would otherwise never have known that they were there. It fell in lines of swarming sparks, catching a dead mouse in the filth on the flagstones, a newspaper that had once stopped the draughts around a window, one of the great, tubular constructions that spiders create when left to themselves, the tall man in the tight trousers who was normally hidden by the shadows at the bottom of the stairs.

Andrew stood in the hallway and inspected the man: the grey hairs curling through the bars of black on his red cheeks, the long coat and the shirt that bunched into frills at his neck. He had dark, kind-looking eyes, a bit like Mr Gwynne's, and around him there were lawns so green that they might have had a light of their own. Glass gleamed in the windows of the house, the frames neatly painted, while pink and yellow flowers bloomed around the walls.

The world in the picture was a place that Andrew recognised, even as he recognised the vague, shadowy world in his little mirror. It was Werndunvan, but it was another Werndunvan – without the crumbling barns and the heaps of machinery rusting round the edges of the yard. It made him think about rolling in the grass, when the spring came over the valley, about Penllan, bright and clean across the hill, and as he looked more closely he could even see the track that Philip had bulldozed, winding its way towards the top of Cold Winter.

Looking again at the hall, Andrew wondered if the man on the wall had once lived at Werndunvan, and if sometimes he would climb from his picture and set off up the stairs, treading carefully, wandering down the passages and into the rooms where grass and saplings grew between the floorboards. He looked at the darkened doorways around him, the sagging cobwebs stretched between the banisters, the stripes of the sunlight, the layer of dust that lay across the jumbled footprints in the corridor that led to the big room, and suddenly he remembered the ghosts that Robin had told him about: the people who stayed in their houses after they were dead, who were horrible and see-through and wanted to kill you.

Perhaps, Andrew thought, this was why Philip and Dora never came into this part of the house, why they had sealed up the door from the lounge and had left it to the rain and the wind. Quickly, he shoved his hand into his pocket and slid his fingers between the cushion and the little mirror. He looked at the shadows near the top of the stairs, the drifts of the dirt, but he was much too scared now to look back at the picture – in case the man was no longer in his frame, or his eyes were no longer dark and kind, but narrowed, horrible, yellow with cruel thoughts.

* * *

For some minutes, Andrew lay on the doorstep, shivering, while Di whined and nuzzled him and occasionally returned to scratching herself. He stroked her sides like they were still covered with hair – not bald and pink with scabs and groups of red, bloody lines – and he talked to her in a language of his own, inhaling the smells of sunlight and the sheep-dip behind the barns, the reek that leached from her skin.

Although Andrew knew by now that his puppy had mange, he pretended to himself that she had been shorn along with the sheep, her coat taken to the huge, sheep-smelling warehouse where he had gone one day with his father instead of going to school, where there were giant stacks of wool that touched the roof and their whole farm's contribution had been lost in moments among the fork-lift trucks and the shrinking aisles of lights. It was a happy time of year to be hairless, after all, when even his father went outside from time to time without his jacket.

Around the doorstep, there were many sounds Andrew began gradually to notice. Above him, a pair of swallows were swooping in and out of a broken window, chattering, delivering insects to their squeaking offspring. Across the yard, a crowd of bantams and chicks were pecking at the dry earth, while a thrush was singing in a nearby beech, and behind the barns Philip and Stuart were driving several dozen ewes into a long, deep trough full of noxious chemicals – dunking them so that everything apart from the sheep itself was exterminated, before pulling out the bung and allowing the poisonous activity to continue in the fields and the streams the whole way down the valley.

Stuart was the son of John the Glyn, and although Philip cursed him continually whenever he was working at Werndunvan, he was one of the very few people who spent more than half a day on the farm at a stretch. Stuart was eighteen years old, kept his hair slicked back like something off the television, drove a scrambler motorbike and wore a ripped leather jacket which Andrew admired and his father mocked mercilessly.

Andrew slunk around the bottom of the barns and sat down against the weatherboarding, among the dogs, on the edge of the area where Philip had once decided to build the new shed. He kept his eyes beneath the peak of his cap, stroking the sole patch of hair that remained on the back of Di's neck, letting his mind drift over thoughts about Robin and Martin, about Tara and the big, clean house. There were only a couple of sheep left in the first of the two pens, wild-eyed and shivering in spite of the constant heat, and he didn't like to watch them struggling to keep their heads above the filthy liquid, scrambling half-drowned onto the earth at the far end.

"Alright, Andy?" said Stuart, when they were finished, wiping his hands on his vest. "How's school, eh? Learning your numbers, are you?"

"Ar," said Andrew, nodding.

Andrew liked Stuart. He liked the way that he smiled and asked him how he was, the way that he wandered about the place as if he was hardly scared of Philip at all, whistling tunes and smoking cigarettes from a smart black packet. Sometimes Stuart would even bring him a present – a chocolate bar or an old toy car – and Andrew treasured these things, hiding them in a hole in the barn, taking them out occasionally to nibble a piece of chocolate or to drive the car around a patch of the hard earth floor.

"Got some mates there, have you?" Stuart continued.

"Ar," Andrew nodded again.

"Who's your best mate, then?" asked Stuart.

"Robin," said Andrew, without hesitation.

Philip closed the gate on the massed ewes, sat on a nearby hurdle and lit his pipe, shaking his head with disappointment.

"Yeah," said Stuart, "and what the fuck's wrong with that? Robin's a nice kid. His dad's alright and all. Ain't done you no bloody harm, has he?"

Philip continued to shake his head, watching one of the swallows as it swept around the nose of the barns, down the fields towards the pond, the pine wood, the big dark hills and the small light clouds that were speckled across the sky. "Can't trust him," he said eventually. "Can't bloody trust him, can you?"

"I'd trust him before I'd bloody trust you!" said Stuart.

"Well, more fool bloody you!" said Philip. "More fool bloody you! Just you try and do bit of business with him, and you'll see... You try and sell him a cottage, look, see what happens then! You won't get your bloody money, I'll tell you that much!"

"And you owe me a few quid when it comes to that."

"And I'll give it you," said Philip. "I'll give it you, don't you worry. Wouldn't want to keep you from getting a nice new jacket, would I? Seeing as how you went and chopped up that one with your mother's fucking nail scissors..."

Andrew had retreated now back beneath the peak of his cap, watching the bits of straw on the earth in front of him, rubbing his fingernails over the mirror in his pocket. The heat and the smell of the sheep-dip made him feel giddy, and the voices of Stuart and his father circled his head like angry flies.

"The fact is," Philip went on, in measured tones, "you come from off, sooner or later you'll be back off again, and that's the truth..." He puffed on his pipe and let the smoke out slowly, obviously beginning to enjoy himself. "Sooner, from what I've heard."

Stuart took a breath like he was about to reply, but Andrew heard nothing further beside the protests of the sheep, the click of Stuart's cigarette lighter.

"Alright, then," he said. "What the bloody hell are you on about?"

"The news," said Philip. "What I've heard is that they're off again, back to wherever the bloody hell they come from... Not good enough, our school, is it? Not bloody good enough! They've got to go and find somewhere else for their precious children!"

"That right?" said Stuart, without great conviction. "And where did you hear that, then?"

"Joe," said Philip, perfectly composed. "And Joe got it off Margaret Hughes, and Margaret got it off her boy, Oliver, who got it off one of Adam's boys, so..." He turned to look at Andrew. "You'd best fucking watch yourself, hadn't you, boy? Your mate Robin ain't going to be around an 'ole lot longer, is he, eh?"

Stuart flicked his cigarette disgustedly into the carcass of a thresher in the weeds, and swaggered down the hill towards his motorbike. When Andrew peeped out from beneath his cap again, there were thin lines of triumph around Philip's eyes and mouth. He tipped his pipe upside down and tapped it on the bar beside him, scanning the dogs until his eyes arrived on Di, sitting on Andrew's lap, scratching at her thin, torn sides.

"I'll tell you another thing," he said, climbing down from his hurdle. "That is the most mangiest fucking dog I have ever seen in my fucking life!"

He picked up Di by the tuft of hair on her neck and swung her out above the sheep-dip, letting her go so that she vanished with a splash beneath the surface. A moment later, she was paddling back towards the nearest end, but Philip took the stick and prodded her around so that she swam towards the second pen, where the sheep began milling and panicking. She swam instinctively, her nose above the chemicals, gasping at the stinking air until her paws touched the slope at the end, where she crawled up pitifully onto the bare earth, pink and shining, and crept off into the shade to lick herself clean.

\* \* \*

Half an hour before they all went home, Mr Gwynne would sit on his desk, swinging his legs, and read the class a story, and that day it was all about King Arthur and his hunt for a boar named the Twrch Trwyth. The Twrch Trwyth had once been king of Ireland, but it had been transformed by God on account of its appalling crimes and, together with its seven wild piglets, had taken to charging round the country, laying waste to towns and villages with its scything tusks and poisonous bristles.

Mr Gwynne had a map of Wales which covered most of the blackboard, and once the Twrch Trwyth had crossed the sea to Pembrokeshire, he began to follow its progress with a length of bamboo and a series of little coloured markers, jabbing excitedly at towns like Milford Haven and Lampester Velfrey. Wales, he explained, had once been a very different place to the way it was today: a wilderness of fathomless forests, of talking beasts and birds that pecked at the stars. The only civilised spot in the whole country had been King Arthur's palace at Caerleon – the finest man had ever seen – and no sooner had news of the marauding boar arrived here than Arthur and his knights were saddling their horses, readying themselves for the chase.

Perhaps the Twrch Trwyth's most peculiar quality was that it had a comb, a razor and a pair of scissors, which it kept between its ears and treasured with such passion that, for all of its wickedness, Robin found himself beginning to like it. Arthur, on the other hand, was always trying to steal them, which didn't quite seem fair. By the time that the two sides met in the Prescelly Mountains, Robin hardly knew which he wanted to win.

"And what do you think the Twrch Trwyth said", asked Mr Gwynne, swinging his legs and inspecting the class over his glasses, "when King Arthur asked it to give him the comb, the scissors and the razor, so they wouldn't have to fight each other any more?"

"'It's bad enough being a huge hairy pig,'" the children chorused, "'without having to talk to you, too!'"

"That's right," said Mr Gwynne. He smiled at Andrew, who had shouted along for the first time. "The Twrch Trwyth really didn't like King Arthur at all. So it waved its snout and it stamped its trotters, and when it charged it was like there was an earthquake, and it scattered his soldiers all the way down the valley..."

There were cars arriving now on the hill outside the school. Parents were gossiping at the gates and the Juniors went pouring through the hall, giggling and shouting. But Mr Gwynne kept on with his story, seeming not to hear the younger children as they started to stir, following only the armies of Britain, Ireland and France as together they pursued the Twrch Trwyth out of Wales and all the way down into Cornwall – scattering bodies and placenames behind them – until, at Land's End, the Twrch Trwyth plunged into the sea and King Arthur seized the comb between its ears at the very last instant, ridding Britain of its wildness once and for all.

\* \* \*

"But I don't want to be the Twrch Trwyth!" Martin complained, as they were sitting in their shorts in the sand-pit outside the school. "Why can't I be King Arthur?"

"Because I'm King Arthur," said Robin.

"And I'm King Arthur next," said Nigel.

"So you've got to be the Twrch Trwyth," said Robin. "Or else there's no one to chase."

"I don't... I don't want to be him!" Martin looked like he was about to cry. "I want to be Sir Kay! I'm telling Tara! It's not fair!"

Beyond the sandpit, which had been reshaped into the Prescelly Mountains, the playground stretched away across hopscotch patterns, improvised goalposts and a large, spiralling snail which nobody had ever quite known what to do with. Through the window of the classroom, Mr Gwynne was reading his book of Welsh mythology, selecting the next day's story, and from time to time he would glance up, checking first the road and then the three boys quarrelling in the sunlight beneath him.

"Come on, Mart," said Nigel. "The Twrch Trwyth won millions of battles, and he did used to be the king of the whole of Ireland!"

Robin looked up at once when he heard the big blue truck, and he watched as it rumbled round the corner of Offa's Bank – fat and filthy through the heat that was shimmering off the road. Turning a tight circle in the junction beside the bungalows, it roared and came to a halt against the pavement outside the school gate, where it idled noisily to itself while Tara tried to open the driver's door and, eventually, climbed out of the window, jumping neatly to the ground.

On the passenger side, Robin could just make out what appeared to be the top of someone's head – the line of a centre parting, the hair shiny and black to either side – and the only person he knew who looked like that was Cloud, so he scrambled to his feet, stretching so he could see if it was her.

"Sorry I'm late, boys," said Tara, wiping her hands on her dungarees as she arrived in the playground. "Hi, Nigel. Everything okay? Hey, guess what, boys! Cloud's here! Mike and Layla have gone on holiday, so she's come to stay for a whole week!"

She picked up Martin's satchel and brushed off some sand, while Robin stared at Cloud, hunched on the seat, her dark eyes focused on her lap and some bits of her hair stuffed into her mouth.

"Hi, Tara," said Mr Gwynne, leaning from the window, removing his glasses. "Everything alright?"

"Fine." Tara picked up Martin from the sandpit. "Thanks for keeping an eye on them... Sorry I'm late. I just... I just got a bit held up."

"No trouble." Mr Gwynne climbed up and sat on the sill, his legs remaining in the classroom. "I was sticking around anyway, and they seemed quite immersed in the exploits of King Arthur."

"And the Twrch Trwyth," said Martin.

"And the Twrch Trwyth," Mr Gwynne agreed.

"Well," said Tara. "Thankyou, anyway..."

She gestured for Robin to collect his bag.

"By the way," said Mr Gwynne, "I meant to tell you. You'll never guess what Andrew's taken to carrying around with him!"

Tara hesitated. She had Martin's satchel held to her chest and she looked oddly uncomfortable, even embarrassed.

"What?" she asked.

"A Claude glass!" said Mr Gwynne.

"A what?"

"A Claude glass!" Mr Gwynne repeated. "One of those little mirrors that tourists used to carry about with them at the end of the eighteenth century, to look at the view?" He paused, as if unsure she was listening, but Tara was watching him with obvious surprise. "They're kind of black and convex. The reflection shrinks the landscape, you see, and washes out the colour, so everything's put tidily in a frame. It's proper picturesque weirdness. People would actually turn their backs to the view and inspect it in their Claude glasses instead..."

"But where on earth did he get it?" Tara asked.

"He said it was just lying about the house." Mr Gwynne shuffled round on the windowsill. His voice was becoming almost tuneful with enthusiasm. "I have to say, Werndunvan is an extraordinary place. You know that bit that they've abandoned. Well, that's an extension built by Thomas Hutchinson, William Wordsworth's brother-in-law! It's an amazing thought, isn't it? All those people staying up there. Dorothy Wordsworth, Sara Hutchinson..."

"What, Asra stayed there?" Tara frowned. "Coleridge's muse?"

"Asra! Exactly! " said Mr Gwynne. "You know about them, then?"

"Well..." Tara slid one of her boots across the tarmac. "Yeah. They were a bit of a passion of mine at one time. Dorothy Wordsworth, Mary Shelley, Mary Wollstonecraft... The major influence, you might say..." She smiled at the dark ground. "But, I can't quite see the Romantics using a thing like Andrew's mirror. I thought they liked their nature untamed."

"That's true," Mr Gwynne nodded. "But, well, a lot of people would have stayed at Werndunvan, I suppose, and they were pretty common things at the time..."

Glancing behind him, Robin noticed that Cloud was peering surreptitiously over the truck door, watching Tara and Mr Gwynne up in the window, so he began to drive his police car furiously up and down the slopes of the sandpit, crashing into Nigel so that he joined in as well.

"You know there's an arboretum at the back?" asked Mr Gwynne. "Thomas Hutchinson built it. I did go up there one time to have a bit of a look around, but..."

"Philip told you to..."

"Yes, Philip told me to..."

The two of them laughed, and Tara released the satchel and allowed it to swing from her hand, inspecting the lines of the playground in front of her.

"Tara?" said Martin. "When are we going home?"

"Just a minute, Mart," Tara said distractedly.

"Can I come back and play, Tara?" asked Nigel.

"Not today, Nigel. There's a friend of the boys who's come to stay, so I'm afraid we're all going to be a bit busy. How about next week, eh?"

There was a pause in which Robin looked from Tara leaning on the school wall to Mr Gwynne perched inside the window frame. The two of them, he realised, were really quite alike. They took the same pleasure in choosing the right word, and they both had a way of telling a story as if they had been possessed by it.

"I don't know if you'd mind," asked Mr Gwynne, "but I would love to see some of your poems..."

"Tara!" Martin repeated.

"Yes, Mart," said Tara. "Okay... Yeah. Um, sorry, Huw, we should really get back. Perhaps we could talk about it some other time. We're in the middle of baling. You know how it is..."

She was looking uncomfortable again, sad even, as the three of them were walking up the playground. She lifted the two boys through the window of the oil-smelling truck, where Cloud was sitting in the middle of the seat, clutching a purple dinosaur on her lap, her hair still buried in her mouth.

"Hi, Cloud!" Robin and Martin greeted her, keenly.

"Sorry you had to wait, Cloud," said Tara. "I got a bit sidetracked. We'll get back up home now, okay?"

"Where's Klaus?" asked Robin. "Is he here, too?"

"Klaus is staying in Llandewi-Brefi," said Tara.

"Oh..." said Robin, wondering how this all added up.

Mr Gwynne waved, but, as she turned into the road, Tara answered with barely a nod. She had the line running down her forehead that Robin had first seen in the barn at Werndunvan, and she drove fast up the hill, so that the engine bellowed and the air rushed round inside the cab, carrying straw and sawdust, baler twine and twizzling bits of wool.

\* \* \*

Down at the ponds, Adam attached some sort of pump to the Fordson, and it began to run night and day, joined by pipes across the former bog, filling the troughs of the animals crowded patiently beneath the trees. Since they were rationing the water from the reservoir, every few days he brought a tank up from the pond to the house, which Tara, Robin and Martin would use to try and coax the flowers back into life, to revive the vegetables and flush the loos of their flies and their stench of bleach and urine.

The best thing to do in this drought, so Adam said, would be to hire a small aircraft or scale a prominent hill, and see if you could make out any prehistoric earthworks among the jaundiced fields. Not that he seemed particularly convinced of this himself: day by day, the sun grew hotter, the higher farms were running out of water, the whole village was gripped by a sense of looming crisis. And Adam kept working through the long July days, from long before Robin and Martin woke up to long after they had gone to bed, the expression hard beneath the wide brim of his hat.

* * *

Robin, Cloud and Martin set off up the hill almost as soon as they got back from school, although Cloud had still not spoken and she looked as if she would rather not have been there at all. For rations, they had four whole meal biscuits and a plastic bottle of milk, plus a pencil and a piece of paper to record their discoveries. To emphasise the seriousness of the mission, Robin had tied them all together with pieces of string, in case one of them fell off a precipice, and the three of them remained tied together as they climbed the gate beneath the chestnut tree, passed the tup in the following field and climbed the gate by the ruined cottage with its new roof and floors, arrows and instructions scrawled across the walls. Then one of the knots came undone and he decided that perhaps the string was unnecessary after all – at least until they had got to somewhere a bit more precipitous.

"We've got a new tepee," said Cloud finally, glancing at the boys to assess its impact. "A proper Red Indians one with a bonfire, and we all play drums and sometimes we do war dances all night until the sun comes up!"

"Well, we've got a new cottage!" said Robin.

"And we've nearly got a tree house!" said Martin.

"Yeah!" said Robin. He paused. It had been some time since Adam had last mentioned it. "Adam's going to make us a tree house soon and tree houses are much better than tepees! So there!"

"No, they're not!" Cloud scowled at him. Her single plait was bouncing against her bottom, her legs brown and spindly in her colourful shorts.

"Robin?" Martin ran a few paces to catch up. "Robin? Are we walking all the way to Cold Winter?"

"Yes, Mart," said Robin.

"Are we going to meet Andrew?" asked Martin.

"Yes," said Robin. "I promised."

For a few moments, they continued to walk towards the fat, green oak tree on the horizon, where the ground fell away towards Werndunvan. The milk slopped rhythmically in Robin's rucksack. The shoots of grass were now long dead on the scar of the old track, eaten by sheep and rabbits and scorched back into the earth, while the grass to either side of them was tall and brown, with faded flowers – daisies, buttercups, dandelions, red and white clover – and the only thing that seemed to be doing well out of the drought were the thistles, which blazed white and purple among the bees and the wasps in the open air.

"Urrgh!" Cloud stopped suddenly. She screwed up her face and stuck out her tongue. "Smelly, horrible Andrew! I don't want to go and see him!"

"He's not smelly and horrible!" said Robin, angrily.

"He's a werewolf!" said Cloud. "That's what Klaus says, and Klaus is nine and you're only seven..."

"You're seven, too!" said Robin. "And Tara says he's not a werewolf, and she's much older, and, anyway, you're just scared because you're a girl!"

Ahead of them, the oak tree was green against the surrounding hillside and the thick blue sky behind the leaves. It was the perfect oak shape, the trunk bulging towards the ground, the branches stretching from as high as the sheep could reach into a great ball of leaves which leant towards the east as if it was doing exercises or about to grab the old Land Rover that was mouldering in the next-door hedge, nettles sprouting through the floor and sheep in the shade beside it.

\* \* \*

Beneath the oak tree, Andrew was sitting, looking upwards at the leaves, which rippled around him and rippled in shadows on the ground, so there was scarcely anything that he could see that wasn't rippling. The leaves were beautiful, with crinkled edges, and he was thinking about those now, stroking the cushion of the little mirror in his hands, listening to the long, dry sighs of the wind – so immersed that he had almost forgotten about Robin and Martin, that they weren't here to meet him like Robin had promised they would be.

When a girl appeared on the stretch of earth where there had once been a track, followed by Robin and Martin, Andrew thought at first that he was imagining things. It was the same girl he'd seen on the day when all the tractors got stuck, her long hair waving behind her like a tail, and it took him some moments to remember why he was sitting here, not back at Werndunvan, by which time the three of them had practically arrived.

"Hello, Andrew," said Robin and Martin.

The girl said nothing.

"You know Cloud, don't you, Andrew?" said Robin. "She was with us that time when all the tractors got stuck, and you and your dad came and pulled them out in the Mercedes four-wheel drive."

"My legs are tired," said Martin. "Robin? Can we have our biscuits now?"

"Where's Di?" said Robin.

Andrew shuffled against the mossy trunk. He glanced down the sharp incline through the gate towards Werndunvan, where the barns that weren't in the old picture blocked the view from the front of the house, the forestry plantation encircled the pair of them and he could just make out the shapes of the dogs in the shadow near the big barn doors.

"In the barn," he said eventually. "She ain't been well. Been in the sheep-dip..."

"Why don't you take her to the vet?" asked Robin.

"I dunno." Andrew shook his head.

Robin put the rucksack on the ground beside him and scrambled up the tree, grasping the twigs that grew from the bulging trunk until he could get up into a fork and from there out onto a branch, where he sat with his legs astride, inspecting the bark in front of him. "There's bracken up here!" he said. "There's little ferns growing, and there's nuts from the squirrels, and there's woodlice everywhere!"

After a while, the four of them pressed through the hole in the hedgerow to reach the common land of Cold Winter. It was only where the hill began to rise again, becoming broken with outcrops, shallow quarries, brambles and rowan trees, that they could see the actual ground. The bracken was a sea the height of a grown-up, waving in the wind, with the tall, thin foxgloves rising above it, bent by the weight of their bell-shaped flowers.

"Do you want to join our gang, Andrew?" asked Robin, as they started down the narrow path. "We need a gang, or else there'll be no one to fight the Sheenah."

Andrew nodded, partly because he had heard about gangs from the television, mostly because he always agreed with anything that Robin said.

"We have to be blood brothers and things," Robin explained. "You can't be a gang without being blood brothers, but we can just do a promise or swap something for now, if you like, because I haven't got a pin here, and you've got to do it properly. You can't just use a thorn."

"Let's play hunting," said Martin, peering out between the fronds at the edge of the bracken. "We can be a team, Cloud, and we can hunt the others all the way over to the quarries!"

Andrew was giggling as they ran through the forest – the high-pitched noise rising from his throat entirely of its own accord. For a time, Martin was chasing him, but he was able to pull away, slipping off down a sheep path where the branches made a tunnel above him, swerving and twisting, where the air was cooler and the ground was patterned with shadows. But the path emerged in a clearing, and there he saw Robin chasing Martin, laughing. So Andrew chased Cloud himself, back into the woods, where suddenly everyone had vanished, and as he ran he thought distantly of dreams in which he had run through the pine plantation with Meg and Di and countless other dogs whom he had never seen before, all of them running together through this world where the light switched roles with the darkness, and when Andrew tripped and went rolling through the tumbling bracken the grass was soft and mossy where he landed.

Robin, Cloud and Martin were sitting in a line on a rock above the bracken as Andrew looked up again, and when Cloud saw him she rolled her eyes right back into her head until they went white all over. For a moment, Andrew felt cold in his stomach, like he felt when the other children were giggling and waving their hands in front of their noses at school. He might have turned and buried himself back into the forest if Robin hadn't gestured to him, turning to look up the last bit of the hill that poked into the hard blue sky.

Pulling himself to his feet, Andrew climbed over the first of the rocks, skirting one of the little quarries where the ewes would go to shelter with their lambs. He followed Robin through a thick band of brambles, listening as he told him about a special door which led into a dungeon somewhere nearby, while Cloud and Martin made their own way up the slope, all four of them aiming for the hilltop.

Andrew was the first to arrive at the top, and he sat down to look at the view. From here, he realised, he could see all the way down to Werndunvan on one side and he could make out the back of Penllan as well, on the corner where the hillside began to turn towards the village. He had never been anywhere where he had been able to see both houses before, and he turned from one to the other, thinking as he looked at Penllan that, if he were somehow to turn back to Werndunvan in that precise instant, he wouldn't see the house that he had left that afternoon, the ragged, colourless place where Di lay shivering in the shadows of the yard, but instead the vivid house in the old picture.

"Our houses, look!" said Andrew excitedly, as Robin appeared a little way down the hill. "Here... Here, you see them both, look!"

"We can use this as a look out point," Robin agreed, taking off his rucksack and sitting down beside him. He shielded his eyes against the burning sunlight. "That way, if the Sheenah attack your house or my house, then we can see them and we'll be in a good place to fight them, too."

Past Cloud and Martin, who were sitting on a big flat rock a few yards beneath them, Andrew could see the still-green sweep of the bracken on Offa's Bank, the rowans on its side, the lessening hills and the plain of England. He could see the wall of the mountains to the south, the balers in the dry brown fields of the valleys, the waves of yellow leading off into Wales – lightening, when he looked at them in the little mirror, until there was nothing to tell them from the sky.

"Can we have our biscuits now, Robin?" asked Martin, looking up at him.

"Come up here!" said Robin. "Then we can all have our biscuits together!"

"Can't you bring them down here?" said Cloud.

"You can see for miles from up here!" said Robin. He was staring at the rock where the two of them were sitting, patches of shrivelled plants around the edges. "You can see miles over Offa's Bank! You might even be able to see all the way to Llanddewi-Brefi!"

"It's smelly up there," said Cloud.

"Tell you what," said Robin, taking the mirror from Andrew's hands and looking in it himself. He handed Andrew the one intact biscuit and put the mirror in the pocket of his shorts. "It's Friday today, yeah? So, I'll swap you the mirror for my rucksack until Monday morning, and I'll bring a pin to school so we can all become blood brothers. I promise. Okay?"

# CHAPTER ELEVEN

# INTO COLD WINTER

It was around about lunchtime on Sunday when Adam finished work on the bottom fields, flicked away the throttle lever on the Ferguson and came striding over to the trailer where Owl was loading up the final cluster of bales. He was wearing a long white shirt which had once belonged to Tara's father, attempting to stave off the sunshine his hat throwing shadows across his sweat-streaked face, the fine white cotton and the intricate stitching smeared with oil and dirt.

"Say what you like," said Owl, settling down against one of the tyres and rolling himself a cigarette, "but this is pretty damned idyllic." He made a clicking noise between his teeth and looked up past the yellow stubble, past the still-green hedgerows where bramble flowers and dog roses spilt between the leaves, the visible ridge of Offa's Bank, until the sun shone straight into his face.

Adam lit his pipe. "Well, we've got some hay, anyway," he said.

"What do you think, kids?" asked Owl, turning to look at Robin, Cloud and Martin, who hadn't moved since he had dismantled their den of bales from around them. "You three going to be farmers when you grow up?"

"I'm going to be a witch," said Cloud, "and I'm going to put a spell on you and turn you into a toad!"

Owl nodded, puffing smoke.

"What about you, boys?" he asked.

"I'm going to be a vet," said Martin.

"I think I'm going to be King of Wales," said Robin, after a moment's thought. "That way, I can live in Caernarvon Castle and have a trebuchet and dungeons and a whole mountain full of treasure!"

Ever since he had reappeared, a couple of weeks earlier, Owl had hardly been asleep at all in the daytime. He had worked with Adam all the way through haymaking, becoming red and then brown, sitting on the lawn at sunset instead of sunrise, rebuilding the cottage when he had nothing else to do and, if he ever tried to stay in bed in the mornings, Robin and Martin were allowed to go and tickle his feet. Because it was always so hot, he only ever wore boots and shorts, and right across his back there had appeared a web of tattoos: foreign-looking writing, fire-covered monsters and cross-legged women floating above snow-topped mountains.

Robin, Cloud and Martin were perched on the bales as the trailer returned up the hill – the tawny valley rising from the leaves of the wood, the earth in the gateways dusty and riven with cracks where it ought to have been muddy and rutted. Robin watched Tara on the Fordson in front of them. He watched Adam on the Ferguson a little way back down the hill, bumping and swaying through the pale grass, the baler and the bale-sledge slithering behind him, a pair of long shadows running down to the ends of his mouth, his head turning slowly to check the sheep in the shade of the hedgerows, his eyes invisible beneath the brim of his hat.

"Last year we all went to the seaside," said Cloud. "We went in a bus. Everyone in our house! Fifteen people! We all went to the seaside together and we stayed in a nice big house next to the beach..."

"You've been to the seaside?" asked Martin.

"Yeah," Cloud sounded surprised. "Haven't you?"

"Of course we have," said Robin. "You probably just don't remember, Martin, because you were too young."

"Anyway," said Cloud, "we all went to the seaside in Pembrokeshire. We played on the beach every day, and we went riding on ponies and everything! But then Mummy had an argument with Jason because he wouldn't wear anything, so me and Klaus and Mummy and Daddy had to go home."

The trailer rolled and heaved with the lumps of the field, and Tara began to steer at an angle across the slope, making an arc to bring them in straight to the gate beneath the big shed.

"How come Klaus didn't come and stay with us, then?" asked Robin. "How come you came and Klaus didn't?"

"Klaus stayed at home," Cloud explained. "He's allowed to because he's nine and he's a boy, and I'm not allowed to stay at home if there's only Judy and Jason looking after us."

"But how come your parents have gone away at all?" said Robin, knowing he was starting to push her. "How come they've gone away on holiday and they didn't want you to come with them?"

As the tractor slowed, Owl jumped down from the top of the stack behind them and opened the gate so that the cavalcade could lurch back up into the yard. They stopped on the enormous boulder that Robin had once persuaded himself was a meteorite, and, as he climbed down the back stay with Cloud crying behind him, he made himself think about the boulder travelling through outer space, about how different it might have looked if it had been carrying a Fordson Major, a trailer and an entire load of bales at the time.

Tara left the tractor idling and, rubbing her hands on the back of her dungarees, she collected Martin from Owl's hairy fingers and lowered him to the ground.

"Cloud!" she said, as she turned back to the trailer. "Cloud, what on earth's the matter? What's happened?"

"Robin—" Cloud was sobbing uncontrollably, tears streaming down her dark face. "Robin... Robin said my mummy and daddy have gone away... He said my mummy and daddy have gone away because they hate me!"

"Robin!" Tara turned to him with such fury that he instantly began to cry as well. "Robin, is this true?" She gathered up Cloud in her arms, pools of a nasty, greyish colour underneath her eyes. "Cloud," she said, softly. "Listen to me, okay? Robin was just being nasty, and he's going to say sorry... Your mummy and daddy have gone away because they need a little bit of time to themselves, that's all. They just need to sort a few things out. Grown-ups get like that sometimes... It's nothing to do with you, okay? Believe me. Your mummy is my oldest friend. I know her better than anyone, and I know that she and your daddy love you and your brother, and each other, more than anything else in the whole, wide world!"

\* \* \*

The dogs were dozing in the shade as Tara and the children crossed the yard on the way to the kitchen to make lunch, their tails stirring up dust, which occasionally caused them to sneeze. Up on the beams of the hayloft, the farm cats were watching the world through half-closed eyes, while the bantams pecked busily at the dust outside the granary and this year's swallows made their first clumsy flights from the eaves of the workshop.

All of the doors of the house were open, as were all of the windows, but the fusty smell of bleach and urine continued to linger in the kitchen. Cloud climbed miserably up onto the bench next to Martin and Robin, the air cool against the thick stone wall where the sunlight hadn't penetrated since the days of George II, a wasp whining on the flypaper in the middle of the ceiling, and the three of them watched as Tara picked up the kettle from the Aga – still blazing away in its cavity – weighed it in her hand, then placed it on the hotplate. She took a scoop of Swarfega from the tub on the windowsill, rubbed it thoroughly into her hands, scrubbing at the grime with her fingernails, then she turned on the tap.

Somewhere deep inside the hill, among the labyrinthine passages, the communities of moles, rabbits, minotaurs and slumbering Welsh monarchs, there was a distant gurgling noise – very much like a monster clearing its throat – and, after a second, Tara sank forwards, wrapping her hands around the back of her neck regardless of the Swarfega, groaning faintly, until her head was almost in the washing-up bowl.

On the bench, the three of them continued to watch her, her white-blonde hair spread among the plates, a pair of smudged handprints on her hips, conscious that a crisis had now been reached and unsure what they could do about it.

"Isn't there any water, Tara?" asked Martin.

Tara didn't move and, for a moment, Robin remembered the big old room at Werndunvan, where the dust lay in waves on the floor, the dry rot pored through the beams and there were no concerns of any kind.

"No," she said, eventually. "On top of everything else, there is now no fucking water."

Tara headed back down the yard in silence, the children scuttling behind her, saying nothing, barely even looking at one another. Poking out from between the haystacks, the bonnet of the truck was streaked with dirt and bantam shit, and they could hear the spluttering of the bale elevator long before they arrived at the big, open doors, where its noise redoubled, booming inside the roof until it seemed to surround them.

Up in the hayloft, Adam had removed his shirt and was working now in a vest and a pair of shorts, while Owl loaded the bales from the trailer onto the patched wooden rungs of the elevator, which carried them haltingly into the air, and no matter how fast Owl put them onto the bottom Adam could still unload them even faster from the top, carrying them to the back wall and stacking them neatly, returning in time for the next.

Tara stood with the three children in the big metal doorway, and her face was hard and brittle-looking.

"Adam!" she called.

"That was quick!" said Owl, smiling, gathering another bale from the trailer.

Adam looked over the edge, then he signalled to Owl to stop the motor and the bantams seemed muted in the silence that came afterwards. He looked at them again, then he swung round the outside of the nearest pillar and shinned back down to the ground.

"What's up?" he asked. "What's happened?"

"The water's run out." Tara pulled her cheeks tight as if the rest of her face was smiling. Adam looked at her for a second or two, then – to Robin's surprise – he put his arms around her shoulders, Tara tipped her head forwards against his neck, and for several seconds they just stood like that. You could smell Adam even from where Robin was standing – the oil, the dirt, the unwashed sweatiness of him.

"Don't worry, my love," Robin heard him murmur, when he finally looked at her again, his voice low and soothing. "We've been careful. It shouldn't have run out yet. I'll sort it out, okay? There's got to be a reason..."

* * *

The ruined cottage was not particularly ruined any longer. It had acquired a smart new fence around the damsons, a roof of shiny Snowdonian slate, a front wall, doorways and window frames, even a swirling, colourful sign which was hanging on the gatepost – pretty well everything you could expect from a cottage.

As Adam, Tara and the children came through the gate from the field behind the house, a crowd of bullocks scattered from the trough in the boundary hedge, retreating a little way down the slope and watching them, flies around their eyes, tails flicking and their shadows on the field beneath them.

Adam stared, looking at the animals with disbelief.

"That fucking–" he growled. He hurried down the hill and turned a tap on the side of the trough. "I'd closed the valve! I'd closed the fucking valve! That fucking man must have put his fucking cattle–"

"What's happened, Tara?" said Robin. "Tara?"

His fists clenched, Adam strode back up the hill towards the scar of the old track, scarcely distinct from the dead grass around it, and stopped at the concrete slab of the reservoir: a spot that a man from Abberton had dowsed for in the days after they had first bought the farm. Grabbing the handle, Adam lifted the lid with one hand, lowered it to the ground beside him and squinted down into the hole.

"Well, Robin," said Tara, hesitantly. "I'm afraid that Philip might have moved his cattle from his pond to the trough on our reservoir. But, maybe it's okay, maybe there's still some water left..."

"Robbo," said Adam, looking up, his voice once again measured. "Do you think you could do us a favour?"

"What, Adam?" asked Robin.

"I don't think I'm going to fit down there, and we're going to need someone to have a bit of a look. There's just a few rungs in the wall on the side, there. It's not very deep."

The reservoir was the coldest place that Robin had been in several weeks, and even with the open lid its blackness seemed to have something of the labyrinth about it, something of the machinations of the inside of the hill. He descended the ladder slowly, feeling for the damp, rusty metal with his bare feet and standing squarely on each one before he felt for the next. Before long, he began to be able to see the walls to either side of him, and he saw that the reservoir really wasn't very big, although glancing over his shoulder he could still see no trace of the back wall and thoughts in the corners of his brain continued to speak of tunnels, undiscovered recesses and caverns full of treasure.

With the final rung, Robin put his foot through a thin skin of water, then a layer of mud, and landed on solid concrete. He glanced back up at Adam, but the small round hole in the ceiling was as bright now as the sun, and not only could he not see Adam's face, he couldn't see anything around him, either.

"What's down there, Robbo?" asked Adam.

"Lots of mud," said Robin.

"Anything else? There should be a pipe sticking out of the wall next to the ladder. Can you see a pipe there?"

Robin bent down and, squinting through the after-images, he saw that there was indeed a pipe sticking out of the wall beside him, and that on the pipe there was a fat frog, its head and back shining green in the startling sunlight, its eyes blinking periodically.

"There's a frog," said Robin. "Quite a fat one. Do you want me to catch him?"

"No, I shouldn't worry," said Adam.

\* \* \*

By the time that Robin arrived back at the top of the ladder, Adam was walking away down the scar towards Penllan, and, while he was moving unhurriedly by anybody else's standards, by Adam's standards he was practically sprinting. Robin pulled himself back out of the dark hole and stood on the heat-shimmering hillside, shivering slightly, the flesh cold beneath his skin. On the bank in front of him, Tara had sat down and was staring towards the ponds with Martin hanging onto her leg and Cloud pressed beneath her arm. Robin scrambled over and curled himself up with them as well, and Tara stroked his hair and told him that he was a good boy for going down into the reservoir, but even with his eyes closed and his head pressed against her side he could still feel the shakiness in her words, and he knew that she was starting to cry.

"It's okay," she was saying. "It'll be fine. This is nothing to do with you kids, okay? Philip is a very strange man, that's all, and sometimes he does things that are a bit difficult for other people to understand..."

Off down the hill, muted by the barns, there was the unmistakable roar of the big truck, punctuated by gear changes, coming and going with the buildings, the trees and the hedgerows, and Robin could see it as it crossed the open fields on the way down to the road – an elbow poking from the left-hand window and the dust rising and drifting over the flat, dry grass behind it.

＊ ＊ ＊

Andrew was cradling Di in the hayloft when he heard the noise of Adam's truck. Scrambling towards an arrow-slit, he knew that something was wrong just by the way that it stopped, the slew of dust that drifted onto the face of the barns. Beneath him, the dogs spilt out of the big, open doors, barking like they had never seen Adam before, and when they did see him they seemed to become confused, retreating in the manner of children, hurling abuse without any one of them stepping forwards to declare themselves the leader.

"Got a problem, is it?" said Philip.

He was fixing the trailer near the top of the yard, dressed as usual in his shirt and dirty brown jumper, and as the engine stopped he got to his feet, wiping his hands on his trousers.

"You listen to me," Adam growled.

Right from the start, the two men seemed to know why he was there, and they faced up to one another with Philip's face as defiant beneath his cap as it had ever been – even if Adam was taller and broader, his muscles daunting as they bulged from his vest.

"I don't know why the fuck you put your cattle on our reservoir–" Adam started.

"My reservoir!" Philip interrupted. "It's my reservoir, it's my fucking field, and it's my fucking business what I put in him!"

"I'm not here to argue with you," said Adam, icily. "You put your cattle on our reservoir. And, I swear to God, if you do anything like that ever again – anything at all that upsets my family – then I'm going to come round here and I'm going to make you regret it for the rest of your fucking life!"

"Upsets my family!" Philip snorted and took a couple of paces forwards, pressing his red face towards him. "Upsets my family?! And how's about my family, eh? Who sent them fuckers round bothering my boy? Eh? That your business, was it? Someone asked you to, did they?"

There was a moment before Adam replied, when even the dogs didn't dare to make a sound. Up in the hayloft, Andrew moved a foot or two away from the arrow-slit, then he crawled back quickly to the heap of bales in the corner, pushed himself into a crack, curled himself around his shivering, bare-skinned puppy and moaned to try and stifle the noise.

"Your boy?!" Adam seemed to spit out the word. "You bastard, you twisted that poor kid till he was barking like a sheepdog..."

"And my cottage!" Philip exclaimed, his voice shaking with outrage. "How's about my cottage?! Who fleeced us out of him, then? Eh? You tell us that!"

"I gave you exactly what you asked for that cottage!" Adam snarled. "You know that as well as I do! If you haven't got the sense to do anything more constructive with your farm than bulldoze the fucking thing flat..."

"Calling me stupid, then, are you?!" Philip was almost shrieking now. "Calling me stupid! Think I don't know what you're up to?! Eh? Think I don't know you're selling up!" He paused and, when Adam said nothing, his voice seemed to swell with triumph. "Call yourself a fucking farmer! Fucking *pussy*, more like!"

Even with his eyes closed and his own voice whimpering in his ears, Andrew could see the two men standing in the bleached yard, between the frosted glass of the kitchen door and the slits in the walls of the barn. He could see Adam, his hands in fists, towering in his boots and his shorts. He could see his father, his face thrust forwards, his bared teeth yellow and broken, squinting in the devastating sunlight.

"Can't take the work, can you?!" Philip taunted him. "Can't take the snow! Can't take the drought! One hard year and you're running away! Fucking pussy!

Or perhaps Radnorshire ain't good enough for you?! Not good enough for you and your precious little boys!"

Through the rising sound of Philip's voice, Andrew heard Adam as he turned and strode away back down the yard. His steps were hard, cutting through the hay and the stone.

# CHAPTER TWELVE

# DARK REFLECTIONS

Andrew woke in the night, and he could feel the pressure of his parents' bodies to either side of him – the rumble of his father's open mouth, the wheezing of his mother. The bed was large but it sank in the centre, and even on these short, hot nights they still used the blankets that they used the whole year round, so that the sweat ran down into the mattress and Andrew's breath became tight in his chest, the air thick and evil-smelling, yellow eyes staring back at him from the windowless walls.

Squeezing between the bars of the bed-end, Andrew slipped out onto the floor and felt for the wall with his hands. The wallpaper was dry and wrinkled. The floorboards were cool through the holes in the ragged carpet. Even in the solid darkness, he liked these feelings, the way that his attention slid towards the ends of his fingers, his toes, his nose, his ears – away from his fading dreams, the wordless things that would surround him and leak into his awareness as the outside world would leak through the absent slates, the broken windows and the dribbling walls of the house.

Andrew dragged his feet as he walked down the passage, clearing the glass and the chippings that had fallen from his father's boots, feeling for the low step up into the kitchen, where he came into a faint shifting orangeness – a light in which he could just make out the table, the chairs placed randomly across the floor, the rubble where the ceiling had come down in the corner, the flickering panes of the filthy window.

Standing in the yard, Andrew sniffed at the warm air flowing towards him. Across the valley, there were lines of fire on the big, dark hills – their movements as slow as the stars. Andrew watched them, fascinated, while the windows of the house shone darkly and an orange haze spilt upwards into the star-spotted sky. Now and then, he held a finger up to his eyes to blot it all out, the way that Mr Gwynne had shown them at school. But he could still feel the smoke in the back of his throat, and when he put out his hand for his little mirror he found instead that Meg was sitting beside him, silently, as though she had been there all along.

\* \* \*

The shadow of Cold Winter still lay thick and dark across the cluster of the house and the barns when Philip called

Andrew for school. Sitting cross-legged in the scattered hay, Andrew tried once more to feed Di from the bottle that they used for the lambs. He lifted her head so that her muzzle pointed upwards, her brown eyes staring towards him, her body cold and limp in his hands, and he murmured comforting noises as he squeezed the pink rubber teat and watched the milk spurt into her mouth, bubbling back up between her lips to make streams that ran between the scabs on her expressionless face. Then he lowered her gently to the floor, while the other dogs watched from the doorway – wary-looking, scarcely seeming to recognise this blotchy-skinned creature as one of their own.

The car bumped and swung as it rolled out of the yard. Andrew clung to his door handle so that he wouldn't bounce onto the floor, and he looked past his father, who was scowling through the dusty windscreen, at the hills across the valley, where the smoke was still rising, drifting over ridges, rocks and the great black smears of the slopes.

"Was it... Was it fire, dad?" asked Andrew, pointing at the hills.

"Ar," said Philip.

"Is it out now?"

"Looks like it, dunnit?" muttered Philip, his eyes on the bulldozed smoothness of the track.

There was still the odd small flower in the fields to either side of them – in the shadow of the hedgerows or in the hollows where there had always been a certain marshiness – but they were faded, and they gave Andrew no more comfort than the few high streaks of the clouds. For an instant, he thought about Di – about how she had stopped shivering, ignoring him when he had tried to talk to her, her eyes clouding over – and he filled his mind with the rainlessness, with Philip and Adam, and how he would soon get his mirror back. And beneath these things were his dreams of the previous night, when he had run through the lines of the pine plantation, when the wind had wheezed in the branches above him and he had vaulted the brambles that coiled from the dry, lifeless earth.

They turned out of the track and onto the lane, which led away down the hill, between the still-green hedges where the ladybirds crawled among the flowers and Andrew had only to reach out of the window to peel the seeds from the long grass. They passed the church and its yew trees, the red telephone box on the corner. They passed the pub, the post office, the bungalows with their neat, parched gardens, the turning to the road that ran behind Offa's Bank to Abberton, and they arrived in the daily crush of cars with the road surface gleaming in the morning sunshine and the shadow of the hillside a sliver that was shrinking by the moment.

Outside of the spike-topped gates, Andrew stood among the legs and the other children, looking out for Robin. He looked anxiously at the big blue truck which was parked beside the road – a metal tank with rusty corners weighing down its back, so that the bonnet seemed to be snarling into the air. He clutched Robin's rucksack, and he didn't want to move in case Tara came out to him on the pavement, as she often did, and held him by the hand as she led him inside.

After a time, there was a gleam of yellow hair in the crowd around the school doors, and Tara emerged in the playground, pausing to exchange a few words with Jim Garraway. Standing in the gateway, Andrew waited for her to turn, to smile and walk towards him, but then he heard a noise to his right and he realised, to his horror, that Adam was sitting in the truck, tapping out his pipe against the hollow metal door. Too scared to think, he shrank behind a gatepost, and as Tara arrived on the pavement she passed so close to him that he could have brushed his hand against her brilliant-coloured skirt.

Mr Gwynne, Andrew noticed, was standing by the classroom wall, turning his glasses in his hands. He was watching, too, as Adam leant from the window, put his arms around Tara's waist and hoisted her up into the cab. For a moment, his face disappeared beneath her luminous hair, his fingers tightening on her shoulders, and the roar of the truck was louder than ever as it moved away up the hill.

\* \* \*

The crowd had shrunk by the time that Andrew turned to go inside. He walked with his head down, his eyes on his dusty brown shoes and the many-coloured lines that crossed one another with impossible complexity in the playground. He didn't look up because he didn't want to see anybody, now Tara had gone, and he looked instead at people's feet: sandals of latticed leather, heels that shrank to a spike at the ground, a pair of neat blue shoes with sun-pink calves, which he followed through the open glass doors – into the hall, where he followed the wall to his peg with its picture of a tractor, where the door to the classroom revealed the room-wide windows, the colourless fields and the web of the deep green hedgerows.

Andrew turned when he heard a pair of voices behind him, although in the classroom a dozen or more children were preparing for assembly, chattering, dragging the mats and arranging the benches in lines. He could smell the hay smell from the fields, the chemicals on the floor, and he was watching as Robin and Nigel appeared from the corridor – smiling and talking, carrying piles of red hymn books.

"Up in the Elan Valley reservoirs," said Robin, "you can see the old church spire coming right up out of the water! That's what Cloud says. And sometimes, at night, you can even hear the church bells!"

"I have got to see that!" said Nigel.

"We're going to go and see it this weekend!" said Robin. "When we take Cloud back home, we're going to go and see the reservoirs, and she's going to show me a barn that's come completely out of the water and normally you can't see it at all!"

The two of them reached the bottom of the stairs and Robin looked in Andrew's direction, but his expression scarcely altered – only his cheeks seemed to flush – and to Andrew it was as if he was looking straight through him, out past the playground, towards the main road and the fading flanks of Offa's Bank – as if he was hardly there at all, like a ghost.

"We're going to stay at Cloud and Klaus's for four whole days," Robin went on, "and they've got a model of a Chinese dragon at their house that looks just like the real thing!"

A bastard – that was what Adam had called Philip. A bastard. And Andrew grasped the rucksack on his shoulder, the hair beginning to prickle on the back of his head, a dreadful fear at the bottom of his stomach. Call me a bastard, would you? Philip had been shouting as Adam climbed back into his truck. Come on, what's the matter with you?! Call yourself a farmer! You fucking start it! Andrew remembered the sound as Adam started the engine and simply drove away. He remembered the moment when his puppy had turned lifeless in his hands, the prickling spreading down his spine, across his shoulders, up onto his scalp until he felt like he would explode. And, as Nigel pushed past him, all he really wanted was for Robin to look at him properly, as if he existed at all.

* * *

On the regular black-and-white squares of the floor, Andrew lifted his head, unable to remember what had just happened. There was a pain in his leg and a thumping in his skull, which made his thoughts leaden and confused. He looked around him and saw hymn books in their dozens – some of them lying neatly, while others were crumpled and ripped – and beyond the hymn books Nigel was curled against the shoe-cages, howling and cradling his arm, while a little further away Robin was crying too, staring at him, and there was blood in streaks on his torn white T-shirt.

Andrew looked into his memory and found little but a dark, swilling emptiness. His fingers were sticky, clenched around a small, familiar object, and there were pieces of glass in his hand. He didn't feel upset, merely concerned for Robin since his bleeding did seem quite bad and he thought that perhaps he should try and do something to stop it. But then Mr Gwynne came running out of the classroom, and Andrew realised that the pain in his leg was very bad, and that he had cuts on his hands, so he began to cry as well.

"What on earth..?" demanded Mr Gwynne, his voice trembling.

"He attacked us!" Nigel wailed. "He was grabbing that stupid mirror, and he bit my arm! We didn't do anything, he just attacked us!"

"Oh, Jesus..." said Mr Gwynne.

"He was like an animal!" Nigel continued.

Mr Gwynne looked quickly at all three of them, then he bent down next to Robin and, talking to him quietly, he peeled off his T-shirt to reveal a long, thin cut across his stomach – not serious, but with blood leaking nastily from several places. The entire class was now assembled in the doorway beside them, and as the first of the Juniors arrived on the steps Mr Gwynne despatched him to find the first-aid kit, talking quietly as he turned his attention to Nigel.

"Look!" Nigel was insisting. "Look – he bit me on the arm!"

"Andrew." Mr Gwynne turned to him, finally. "Andrew, are you okay? What on earth just happened?"

Andrew looked up at him, sitting upright now, but he couldn't seem to make any sense of the words that Mr Gwynne was saying, so he simply looked back at the teacher's face, at the eyebrows bunched together, the dark, rumpled hair. Then he decided to lie down again and close his eyes, and there, despite the heat, despite the reek of the chemicals on the floor beside him, despite the commotion, the crying and the shouting, he could still smell the smells of Werndunvan: the sleepy dogs arranged between the big, open doors, the pots bubbling tirelessly on the Rayburn, the fragrance of the hay, the sunlight piercing the holes in the roof of the house, drying out the mould and the grass which had once been trying to grow there.

\* \* \*

There was a path in the garden that only Andrew knew about, and it was so narrow and tortuous that even he had to crawl to follow much of it – sliding beneath the trunks of fallen trees and squeezing between their branches. The garden was a fantastical place, full of plants which gangled high into the air while their roots scrabbled outwards over the soil, as if they had no interest at all in going underground and were more interested in communing with the shrubs, with the eruptions of purple flowers and the clusters of earth-brown bull rushes.

In the middle of all this wilderness, there were people made of stone – some of them without fingers or faces, others sinking slowly into the earth while their hands reached upwards into the dark, fleshy foliage. As he crawled among them, Andrew imagined that this was an entirely different kingdom, that he was a king who had returned to his country, and he pictured himself in his rightful palace, the finest that man had ever seen, seated on his throne, tending his sheep, which were boundless and had never lost a lamb.

Beyond the house, far behind him, there were the sounds of cars in the yard. Unfamiliar voices were shouting Andrew's name – calling for him at intervals – and when a twig caught the bandages wrapped around his hands, he pulled them off quickly and left them lying on the ground.

The path ended at the edge of the plantation, having tunnelled for several yards beneath a bank of flowering brambles. Andrew returned to his feet, brushed some of the dirt from the front of his shirt, his jacket and his trousers, and sniffed at the resinous smell in the air, the order and the shadows. Then he set off briskly down the hill into the narrow little valley which ran beside the house, dodging the oil drums and the plastic crates, murmuring a tune to himself while the lines of the pines shrunk off towards the bottom of the world.

There was a pool at the head of the dingle, which was Andrew's favourite place on the whole farm. Beside it, there were a pair of seats cut back into the slope: levels of moss-covered rock, girdled in white and yellow flowers, and so old, so worn, that they might have belonged to the house itself.

Andrew sat on one of the seats and he imagined that Di was sitting on the other. Once the spring had cascaded from the hillside, but now it was just a bowl of cracked earth with a puddle in its middle scarcely larger than his hand. He watched as an insect danced on the surface of the water, and as he watched he took the little case from his pocket, slid open the clasp and ran his fingers across the place where there had once been a mirror, where there was now just a space of brownish metal. The circles spread from the feet of the dancing insect, round and perfect, growing as far as the puddle would allow. They were green from the layers of the trees, blue from the sky, brown from the earth, and as Andrew watched them he felt the vague, dizzy feeling rising up in him until, after a time, it was as if there was nothing but these circles in any direction, spreading away from him as far as he could see.